JOHN EDMISTON

UJUNG KULON

Waitapu
LONDON

First Edition
2010

Published by Waitapu Publishing
PO Box 446
Twickenham
TW1 9HU
United Kingdom

www.waitapu.com

All characters in this book are fictitious
and any resemblance to persons
living or dead is purely coincidental.

A catalogue record of this book is
available from the British Library.

ISBN 978 0 9565254 0 6

CONTENTS

Ujung Kulon

THE VOLCANO

It had been two days since he had left the capital. Now the dark shape of the island was once again before him in the distance, its cone of volcanic ash jutting out from the sea like the head of a gigantic whale surfaced from the depths. Wisps of smoke plumed from the smouldering crater into the still of the tropical noon. Standing in the ship's bows, Mitchell could already detect faint traces of the volcano mingling with the light sea breeze. He breathed in deeply, savouring the familiar mixture of sulphur and salt. It seemed to welcome him like an old friend. Each breath that filled his lungs ignited half-forgotten memories and ancient images that curled like vapour, up from the core of his being. But he had other memories which lay closer to the surface, memories it would be impossible to even half-forget.

Only eight months before, he had spent several days on the volcano and the surrounding islands of the submerged crater rim. It had been the initial stage of his reconnaissance of the area before moving on to explore the jungles of the mainland.

He recalled that first day when they had approached the island.

* * *

The continuous rumbling had been deafening. Even from twenty kilometres away they'd had to shout at each other to make themselves heard. Explosion after explosion had echoed across the narrowing expanse of water. A great column of black ash towered into the sky. Looking through the lens, Mitchell had watched in awe as the volcano flung huge boulders effortlessly into the air, curving slowly to plummet into the ocean with an audible hiss. Long sprays of molten magma were lobbed in delicate arcs of trailing smoke, flicking tufts of ash from the steep slopes where they landed.

It had been Dominique who had insisted they go ashore. He had wanted to, of course, but the violence of the eruptions precluded him from even suggesting it.

Filming from the boat had already provided footage that he knew was unique. He experienced an almost tangible charge while shooting such sequences. Moments of near trance-inducing wonder seemed to unfold before him, in which some charmed serendipity between camera and subject allowed an almost precognitive anticipation of those unrepeatable fragments of time. Such moments of interaction, funnelled through the view-finder into his eye, seemed to reveal a new and enlarged dimension of being, a sense of connection in which exhilaration and calm alternated in a fragile co-existence. He hungered for the images that triggered this elation. They were like food. It was to experience such moments that Mitchell filmed.

Dominique had been determined they land on the volcano. She wanted to record at close range and full volume the sound of the upheaval. Mitchell took chances, but this time, looking up at the maelstrom of raw primal power before him, even he couldn't rationalise the risk. As the boat chugged closer to the island they had screamed and shouted at each other, arguing above the din. She had kept on insisting. Dominique, when determined, was hard to ignore. She knew that if she persisted, the solid dams of reason and commonsense in which Mitchell harboured his arguments would eventually start to crack, and a tide of powerful obsessions and unspoken motivations would flood his judgement. It was these obsessions that had brought them to this shore.

He was compelled by a need to create an entirely new generation of wildlife programme - films in which the forces of nature were shown as they were; raw, destructive, unsanitised - that didn't baulk at showing dismemberment or death, disease, pain or parasites. His were films that confronted their suburban audience - oblivious of the vicissitudes of nature - with a harsh reality; films that glimpsed the natural world as a brutal slaughter-ground where hunger-tormented creatures battled for everyday survival and where copulation was an unadorned function of instinct. These were programmes unsmothered by wall-to-wall narration or the glib reassurance of a paid actor or wheeled-on expert.

He refused to practise any of the tricks common to other cameramen; artificial set-ups, fenced-in jungles, aquariums disguised as riverbeds, and in particular, the use of bait. For him this was travesty. He wanted films with images that made the eyes bulge; that seared the brain, divested of voice-over and music, enriched only by layers of natural sound.

The films he made showed the planet as it was; cataclysmic, the forces of nature in the throes of constant change, its flora and fauna undergoing a widespread extinction of species.

They had gone ashore.

Mitchell edged the boat's dinghy through the carpet of pumice which surrounded the coast. Undulating against the shoreline in a solid wave, the drifting debris resisted the intrusion like a cushion. Squeaking horribly, the bow scraped against the white floating boulders. He pulled harder, thrusting the oars deep below the surface, forging a channel through to the shore.

Knee-deep in a fine powdery ash, they trudged up the beach to where a few stunted casuarinas clung tenaciously. Dominique placed the twin mics on their stand and switched on the recorder. He set up the tripod and started filming.

The pillar of black dust stretched high above them. The wind had spread a dark pall across the sky. A constant thunder struck his eardrums, entering and echoing within his head, reverberating like a perpetually mounting storm. The island shook with the intensity of the explosions. With every new eruption, massive clouds of dust belched from the cauldron.

Already he had shot an entire roll. He unloaded the magazine and looked up at the mountain of fire. Tongues of molten lava licked the crater's rim. Each upheaval sent streams of viscous magma dribbling from its mouth, cooling as it trickled down the slopes like strands of black igneous vomit. Boulders tumbled down the steep sides of the volcanic cone. To the north, showers of smaller rocks rained down upon the foothills of cinder. Yet that part of the foreshore on which they stood seemed curiously protected from the bombardment. As Mitchell loaded another magazine, an enormous peal of underground thunder shook the earth. From the corner of his eye he saw Dominique throw her head back, the sound of her laughter hidden beneath the roar of the explosion.

He panned from the volcano's summit down over the dunes to where jets of gas and steam escaped through fissures in the ash. Clouds of sulphides drifted towards him. He changed lenses and refocused. Pools of brightly coloured salts, orange, red and yellow, stained the windward margins of each opening. The steam hissed with a moist sibilance. Clumps of crystals grew in the damp interstices, miniature ecosystems in an otherwise arid terrain. He and Dominique climbed towards the steam vents to get a closer look. He set the tripod at a low angle and adjusted the lens. At that moment, the blow-hole started to emit a shrill piercing note, rising in pitch as the underground pressure sought release. The shriek rose to an ear-splitting crescendo as he sharpened the image. Suddenly, a geyser-like spray of gas and boiling vapour spumed with tremendous violence from the fumerole. The clusters of crystals at the lip of the crevice glistened like translucent tusks. Aimed at these strange growths, all the power of the plutonic force seemed concentrated, as if discharging to the quivering crystals an oracle of irrevocable intent. Tilting up the scalding jet, he imagined these emissions magnified by the natural properties of the crystals, transmitting, through this small aperture, an invisible all-pervading code.

Far above him, billions of tons of sulphuric acid were condensing in the stratosphere. Inevitable changes to climate and the patterns of global weather would follow.

He took his eye from the camera and turned to Dominique. She had tossed away her shorts and shirt, and was standing, wearing only her socks, rubbing her breasts. The sight of her looked so incongruous, so dislocated from expectation, that for a moment he felt suspended in some semi-dream. It seemed an age before he again heard the skull-splitting scream of the fumerole.

She stood there, cupping her hands beneath her breasts in a strange fertile gesture. Her lips moved rapidly. He realised she was shouting to him, but above the din of the eruption he couldn't hear a word. It was like looking at some bizarre old film without a sound track, a lost relic of silent cinema unfolding before his eyes on a distant screen, shimmering in heat-haze and sulphurous vapour. She shook her dark mane of hair as if infuriated and suddenly flung herself to the ground. A convulsive thrashing gripped her limbs, pushing her flailing torso into the thick carpet of ash. She writhed wildly, as if determined to burrow deep beneath its surface. Digging with her hands and feet, she threw ash behind her like an animal possessed.

Mitchell wondered if she was having some kind of seizure or an epileptic fit. He went over to where, half-buried, she rolled and shuddered in the white powdery tuff. It clung to the moisture on her dark body in a macabre elemental costume.

He knelt down beside her, remembering the twisted bodies he had seen only a few days before, lying sprawled by the side of the road as the tanks, their exhausts roaring in his ear, had rolled up to reinforce the embassy. In the confusion, a rooster, freshly liberated from a nearby market, had run across the square, looking for all the world as if it were terribly late for an appointment, strutting between the APCs and the gathering groups of soldiers, heading straight towards the mangled remains of the embassy gates as if it alone still retained a clear sense of purpose in this sea of chaos. For a few suspended moments it looked as though the rooster had seized the very stuff of history and had arrived just in time to oversee what needed to be done.

Wearing dark glasses, impassive beneath his helmet, a sergeant had stepped forward, took slow and careful aim, and with one shot blasted the bird to a flutter of feathers.

Through the shards of thought that sprayed through his mind he remembered thinking that this sense of chaos gone mad, ultra and extreme, beyond all reason, seemed to follow him wherever he went, as if he himself might in some way have been the guilty catalyst for the horror he saw all around. Yet here, where corruption, tyranny and a complete absence of accountability had festered for so long, he felt he was witness to the birth of a new type of evil, bred only for hatred and escalating revenge, a pure form whose incubation was now at an end.

It was then that the second explosion had ripped apart any attempt at comprehension.

He felt the rush of air on his face. People fell all around him. In the screaming tangle of bodies, Dominique had lost her balance and slipped. He saw her disappear behind a wall of stampeding feet.

"Dominique !"

A young man, clutching his stomach had staggered by.

He glimpsed her briefly, crumpled in a heap, and rushed over to where she lay.

"Dominique !"

He heard a low moan.

"Dominique ?"

The whole island shook in the grip of another massive upheaval. He looked up to the summit. Projectile fragments of molten rock shot from the crater and hurtled towards them.

This terrible beauty somehow compelled him.

Here was an energy whose enormity dwarfed human endeavour; here was a realm in which death seemed less dangerous than a life without risk. He felt he could understand his war-correspondent colleagues, unable to live without the constant proximity of death.

He looked down.

Rising to her knees, Dominique shook so violently that she seemed animated only by the spasms that seethed through her limbs. They jolted involuntarily, twitching like drowning fish. Her feet kicked and twisted, her arms threshed through the dust. In a frenzied series of lurches, her whole body heaved and contorted, then shuddered and was still.

"Dominique ?"

He heard another low moan from under her matted shock of hair.

Crouching motionless in the dust before him, she looked like some mythic creature, half-woman, half-lion, sprawled out on a desert wasteland, a guardian of secret knowledge. He closed his eyes. Amidst the tumult all around, he experienced a calmness, like that at the eye of a cyclone, so delicate he sensed even his thoughts might disturb the equilibrium. At this precise moment in time he knew he was poised as if at a fulcrum, a turning point in the measured direction of his destiny, a rubicon beyond which all bridges must be ceremonially burnt. This was an epicentre from which the ripples of choice would radiate.

"Dominique !" he shouted above the din.

A thunderous explosion ripped through the lesser layers of noise.

Bending on all fours, Dominique thrust her buttocks high into the air.

"Eat me," she screamed; a violent instinctual hunger in her voice.

The words tumbled through his head. He felt his blood quicken, a heavy ache pulsing between his legs, rubbing against the rough cotton of his trousers.

A large lump of rock landed nearby, smouldering.

"Do it, Mitchell, eat me," she screamed, impatiently hurling a handful of cinders back towards him.

"What ?"

"Do it !" she screamed.

He resisted the urge to turn around, to check that some other cameraman wasn't already there, filming for a rival channel the initial patterns of their unexpected courtship.

He looked down. The tufts of hair that adorned her sex were dusted with a fine pollen of white volcanic ash and vermilion earths. Clots of bright sulphurous salts, lodged in the wet knotted tangle, deliquesced and ran like streaks of honey down her thighs. Mitchell knelt behind her. Slowly, he put his mouth to her sex and kissed her. He was surprised how wet she was. He ran his tongue around the sulphur-stained fur, savouring the rare mélange of flavours and the overwhelming bouquet of sex. His mouth began to moisten at the pungent infusion of mineral tastes; salt, acid and brimstone.

Reaching down between her legs, Dominique ripped open his trousers and squeezed him hard.

He heard her moan above the volcano's growl.

"Don't stop," she insisted, "don't stop."

Thunder rumbled from the volcano. Gasping for breath, he looked up at the peak, where sheets of ash were being thrown far into the sky. Far above them, an immense network of lightning crackled within the dark column. Thick clouds of cinder began to float down all around, covering them in a fine dusting of powder. A gigantic peal of thunder violated their eardrums.

Dominique pushed him backwards and sat crouching above him, rubbing hard against him.

What would it matter, he wondered, if he were to die now, swallowed in the volcano's suffocating grip ? It was too late to stop. Perhaps some future generation of geologists would unearth them, coupled in a Pompeian saturnalia, petrified forever *in flagrante delicto.* A scandalous issue would herald his resurrection. It amused him to think he and Dominique might be placed in some museum on public display, their fused statue a monumental icon of perpetual desire.

Spots of rain fell in a thin drizzle. A gesso-like paste of volcanic mud, brought down by the rain, spattered their bodies, patterning them in variegated streaks.

It began to rain harder.

Again Dominique's body started twitching. The torrential downpour lashed at their plaster-coated limbs. A massive bolt of electricity flashed overhead. The thunder rolled almost instantly; its peal and the volcanic eruption merging into one continuous percussive roar. Dominique let out a violent protracted scream and came with a liberating frenzy. As she climaxed, he felt a torrent of spray sluice across his face.

* * *

Later, they walked from the vents back along the dunes. The seismic shudders continued underfoot. Flakes of obsidian gleamed in the dust. Dominique bent down and picked one up, turning it over in her hand, fingering its sharp blade. Sulphurous smelling fumes wafted through pores in the crusted tuff. Mitchell looked through the corner of his eye at the solfataro to his left. Its jagged gash had ruptured an outcrop of andesite and was expelling choking clouds of pale vapour. Trapped in the entrance, a large sea eagle had fallen, its wings outspread; the mineral heat smelting its remains to a shining vitreous mass. He noted the remains of several smaller birds lying in the ash, overcome by poisonous vapour. He realised that he and Dominique had drifted into a valley in which the vitriolic gases were accumulating. As he looked around he saw that Dominique was far behind, standing in the lower hollows, still examining the chunk of obsidian. Sulphides swirled around her legs. He shouted to her. As if awakening from a trance she looked up as he raced towards her. Together, they ran to the nearest dune. Knee-deep in ash, his feet sliding with every step, he half-dragged her up the ridge, scrambling to its crest. There, lungs heaving, gasping for air, they collapsed in the dust and fell into a loose embrace. They lay there in the burning sun, motionless, exhausted. After what seemed like an eternity, he rolled over and found they were perched just yards from the sea. Terns wheeled overhead. He looked out at the vast stretch of ocean and felt the warm salt-breeze waft across his face.

* * *

Back on the boat, they ate their evening meal in silence, looking up, now and then, to the dark outline of the island. Afterwards, Mitchell once again unpacked the camera and loaded a roll of fast film. An intense gold and ruby light had begun to flood the sky as the sun sank slowly into the ocean. Filtered through the dense layers of dust particles, it was the most spectacular sunset Mitchell had ever seen. Small tufts of cloud, like lamb's fleece or the patterns on a bird's wing, burnt a brilliant succession of colours in the upper atmosphere, while below, darker shapes scudded across the sky from beyond the horizon, blown towards them by the prevailing winds, like messengers to an unknown augur.

To the east, a waxing moon rose above the distant land mass. In the short tropical twilight the colours began to glow. A steady splash of wavelets lapped against the side of the boat. Time seemed to dilate. He turned and saw Dominique staring at him, a strange fierce look burning in her eyes.

As the sky slowly faded he looked over the gunwale to where streams of phosphorescence gleamed on the water. Dominique dipped her hand overboard and ran it across the surface; trails of living light blazing in its wake. Again and again her fingers stabbed the water, as if enraged by the tiny glowing creatures. Coating her dripping fingers as she lifted them from the water, they pulsed with a green glow.

The sea around the boat was teeming with organisms.

Busy with a net, Mitchell scooped a sample into a jar so it could be identified back in London. He picked up his camera and opened the lens wide. As he filmed, Dominique agitated the water with a boathook, increasing the visible radiation. The photophores danced like meteors on the waves.

A school of small squid came to observe. Hovering just below the surface, they watched the activity on board with their keenly developed sense of sight. Every time the boathook came too near, they retreated to a safer distance, their tentacles streaming, then approached again, curious for a closer look.

Below the surface, a hydrozoan medusa - a type of bio-luminescent jellyfish - drifted by. Without warning, Dominique lunged forward, the boathook darting in her hand. Deftly skewering the medusa, she held it aloft with an air of savage triumph.

Mitchell continued to film. As darkness fell and the pale gibbous moon rose over the ocean, he turned his lenses to the inky silhouette of the volcano. Tongues of orange fire spurted from the vertex as if it cradled some great subterranean dragon. The lava glowed against the darkening sky.

Lying on his bunk that night he visualised the immense geological forces constantly at work within the earth. Far below him, at the edge of a deep oceanic trench, two slabs of the earth's crust were colliding together. Gradually, one plate was sliding under the other, disappearing into the depths of the trough. As this slab of ocean floor was being slowly ingested, the brittle surface rock descended into the hotter regions of the mantle. There, in a constant furnace, the rock became magma, its convections generating the powerful currents of the earth's magnetic field. Within the flux of this underground smelter, volatile gases and liquids created enormous pressures in the molten rock. Blasted to an incandescent heat, the magma found its way through tension cracks to create a chimney through to the surface, erupting from the volcano's dark truncated cone.

He woke to find Dominique crouched over him, nuzzling the warm hollow in the nape of his neck.

* * *

Dominique. The memory triggered a chain reaction of emotions within his mind. "What happened to you ?" he asked out loud. The Sundanese boat master looked up at him quizzically. In the four months since she had disappeared, Mitchell had turned over every possibility in his mind. There was only one conclusion he could come to. He had to return. He had to know if she was still alive.

At first he had resisted even the thought of going back to the reserve. He had searched for her, week after long week, in those dense palm forests and torpid swamplands. He had enlisted the local guides and conservation staff guards and in small groups they had fanned out across the reserve. In growing desperation, he had radioed the capital and fought a path through the rank bureaucracy until eventually, a Forestry Department helicopter had arrived. Swooping low over the foothills and along the coastal strips they had searched for days, probing the river systems and marshlands until the pilot grew sullen and became unwilling to continue. After ten days of flying, Mitchell had been unable to persuade him from returning to the comfort of his villa. Alone, he had once again slashed his way through the jungle, screaming her name in the sweltering equatorial heat, looking for the smallest clue. Two months later, he still hadn't found a trace of her.

The images of that primeval forest had begun to seep into his consciousness and invade his dreams. For another week, he had lain in one of the palm-thatched guard-huts, exhausted and unable to eat. Animals rummaged around outside the door. Amplified by his immobility, their sounds cast up dark taunting shapes like hybrid creatures gathering in the shadows. Oversized insects with powerful crunching mandibles and long waving antennae approached and rustled around him. Defunct species of the mind transmogrified and crept ever closer. Once, he awoke screaming as a cockroach crawled over him, inspecting the corners of his mouth.

That same night, he dreamed he was encircled by vines, captured in a cocoon-like morsel by a demented tree whose branches waved like the legs of a spider. Hoisted aloft, he hung upside down while large black seeds germinated in his stomach and sprouted through his abdomen, growing rapidly in tropical profusion, their roots reaching down through his arteries to the nourishment in his brain.

Utterly debilitated by fever, he had approached the borderlands of sanity, until finally, sapped of strength, haggard and ill, he had stumbled back to the jetty to await the next boat out.

The visions from that time scarred his memory. He still found it difficult to trust his own mind. Was it really only six weeks since he had left the reserve ? since he had returned to London ? And eight months since he had been here, at the volcano ? He looked up again at its dark shape. It was difficult to believe he was back.

The idea of re-entering that dank forest haunted him. Starting the search here at the volcano was a way of delaying what he knew was inevitable. But now, with its dark silhouette once again before him, beckoning like a secret enemy, he felt an irrational horror at the recurrent cycle unfolding beyond his control.

There was no logical reason to come here again. On the previous trip, they had stayed here only a few days. But the volcano, which had precipitated such primal reactions in Dominique's psyche, had become an implacable challenge to the success of his return. Its dark shape, standing like a gate at the entrance of the reserve, had cast so large a shadow on the substratum of his memories, that he knew he must re-explore its significance. He sought in retracing his steps here, to transmute from the inexhaustible core of the volcano, a talismanic courage with which to enter the now gaping fracture in his own soul, to remould in the deeper vaults of his mind the pyroclastic fragments of being, scattered by the trauma of her loss.

The cone on the horizon was now quiet. He pointed to the small islet to the northwest of the volcano and asked the boat master to head in its direction. It was just possible, he told himself, that she had found her way here, hitching a lift on some coastal freighter, to be near her beloved volcano. Would he find her there, he wondered, clinging to some stark survival, existing on a grim diet of shellfish and lizard ?

The boat chugged towards the neighbouring islets. They were the surviving fragments of the old crater rim; all that remained of the original volcano. It had collapsed into the ocean in a series of cataclysmic explosions that must have dwarfed the activity he and Dominique had witnessed. The resultant caldera was enormous. As they motored over its surface towards the largest of the islands, Mitchell had twice noticed dead fish floating on the surface. One of them, a large silver tuna, was being mauled by a frenzied group of sharks.

The rate at which these islets had re-afforested over the years had been of considerable interest to evolutionary science. Plants had reappeared with an astonishing rapidity. Palms, fig trees, casuarinas, wild sugar cane and orchids had all found a foothold. The larger seeds, such as the *nipa* and coconut palms, must have floated on the currents, while others had probably been borne by birds from the mainland. Traditional theory suggested that the fauna arrived more slowly - bats and birds flying in with the first establishment of vegetation. With no predators they would have found the island an ideal niche. Inevitably, carnivores would have followed, ancestors of the island's small population of snakes, lizards and rats. Yet that theory was now under threat as field studies at other volcanic sites showed it was smaller predators - mites, spiders and beetles, living on tiny airborne prey - that first colonised the sterile wastes. It was their burrowing activity which provided the first suitable niches for much of the vegetation itself to take root.

* * *

Reaching the island, he and Dominique had clambered ashore on a tiny rock-strewn beach. They had walked quietly through the light undergrowth. Almost immediately, Dominique had spotted a reticulated python poised in the lower branches of a fig. It was possible to approach very close to pythons. Mitchell had once filmed a five-metre specimen from just in front of its nose, using only the camera to protect himself from any lunge it might make. Although non-poisonous, it could still give a nasty bite. At that time, he had been so close he had needed to use the macro lens, pulling focus down from its eyes as it flicked its tongue in and out. Larger pythons he treated with more respect; they had been known to crush and swallow humans within a few hours.

Watching the python above them, they had noticed it was slowly edging forward; its gaze transfixed on a point beneath it. It was only then that they had seen the heron, hidden amongst the foliage, perched on a branch below. The heron, a juvenile dusky grey, had its eyes closed and was obviously asleep. Mitchell had set up the camera, attaching three telephotos to the revolving turret-mount. The movement of snakes had always fascinated him.

He took several establishing wide shots with both snake and heron in the same frame, then swivelled the turret-mount to a longer focal-length lens.

The snake slid towards the bird. The python's underside rose and fell in an almost imperceptible series of rippling waves. These minute contractions enabled the rear edge of its underbelly scales to catch onto the smooth bark of the fig, propelling it forward with urgent purpose.

The python's tongue darted in and out, gathering traces of airborne scent. It was now directly above the heron, motionless, its entire attention focused, determining the moment to strike.

What Mitchell needed was a big-close-up of the python's eye. If he took one later, it would never have the same look of intense concentration, the same degree of instinctual drive. He rotated the turret to the longest telephoto. Already he was focusing. The image clarified in the viewfinder. A perfect light brown circle filled the frame. He started shooting. To see this eye in close-up was to enter a new world in appreciation of reptilian beauty. The iris glistened like a jewel, like a gemstone of amber in which a small fragment of prehistory has been entrapped and preserved. Concentric zones of pale colour lay sunken in the depths of its tawny semi-opaque pool. A point of light gleamed in the vertical cleft of the pupil, like a diamond within the entrance of a narrow cave. His attention went to this point of light, rested in it, captivated by its stillness. Here was the focal node of an ancient instinctive intelligence, charged to the extreme of concentration. He felt as if the snake was returning his gaze, staring down the telescopic funnel into the inner reaches of his being. Abruptly, the aperture of the snake's pupil dilated in a final summoning of primordial energy. Staring at this brown bead, he felt reluctant to return to the wider shot. It took an effort of will to change lenses. He only just managed it before the python lunged forward.

The snake dropped with an awful inevitability onto the sleeping bird. They fell in a seething tangle to the forest floor, writhing amongst the leaf-litter and creepers at the foot of the tree. The heron, for one brief second, looked as if it might escape, as both its legs and a wing fought free in a terrible squawking flurry. But within moments, the python had wrapped another coil around the struggling bird, twisting its powerful length in a tightening spiral embrace. Constricting its grip a little more each time the heron exhaled, the snake patiently compressed the bird's fragile life, squeezing with economical effort, the last remaining moments from its crushed body. With one terminal gasp for breath, the heron expired.

He had turned and saw Dominique, her eyes fixed as if in some mantic stare.

"Dominique ?"

There was no response.

"Dominique ?"

A faint flicker registered in a muscle on her face. Her hand began to twitch. She turned towards him. It was such an odd look she gave him that he was taken aback. He recoiled instinctively then attempted to disguise it by pressing his eye to the viewfinder. He hoped she hadn't noticed. He panned back to the snake. The lingering enigma of her look dissolved as the lens came to rest on the sight before him.

To swallow prey that was so much larger than the size of its own mouth, the python had evolved an extraordinary set of jaws. Hinged at the intersection with its skull, they could dislocate completely from their sockets, stretching and expanding to encircle their catch.

He watched as the heron was drawn in head-first, the python's lower jaw extending to a seemingly impossible degree. Soon, all that could be seen was the bird's feet and long wading legs protruding from the serpent's ever-present smile. Then, its flanks distended by an enormous bulge, the python had slid off into the vines and aerial roots that hung in a tangle from the trunk of the tree.

* * *

The loud splash of the anchor interrupted his recollection. The chain rattled against the bow as it slid overboard. The hum of the engine subsided to a low throbbing pulse.

As the boat approached the beach, he felt a wave of discomfort, like a kind of dread, rising from within. This island, with its lush concentration of jungle, had first appeared on the horizon like an image of renascent growth, a microcosmic Eden in which new possibilities had lain concealed. But now its thick, almost impenetrable tangle of thorny palms seemed to echo the barbed skein of his mind as it threaded its way back and forth through time. Yet he felt drawn by some irresistible lodestone of fate to its shore, as if a line of magnetic force to which only he responded, was intersecting at this remote location, a dark complex within his psyche.

He turned to Villiers.

"It was here Dominique twisted her ankle," he said, pointing to the narrow fringe of vegetation that lay beyond the foreshore. "We were carrying the gear back to the boat. Dominique got her leg hooked on some rattan and lost her balance."

"Hmm ... nasty stuff, rattan," concurred Villiers, watching him carefully.

They climbed into the dinghy and started rowing towards the beach.

THE ECLIPSE

Villiers watched the oars dip in and out of the water as Mitchell rowed. Below the surface the occasional flash of coloured fish caught his attention. He looked at the man facing him. Not for the first time on this journey, he noticed Mitchell avoiding his gaze.

When he'd first heard of his wife's disappearance, his work had lost all significance. He had been unable to concentrate on the paper he was preparing. It was his most important paper to date, the culmination of his entire work as a photo-biologist. After years of carefully designed research, studying a wide range of organisms including plants, invertebrates and fish, he had amassed a conclusive body of evidence for specific correlations between bio-luminescence and the rhythms of electro-magnetic tides. He had found that these fluctuations in the magnetic field of the earth - produced by solar and planetary angularities - corresponded, in the light-generating organisms in his study groups, to periods of statistically significant variation, both in levels of luminosity, and in the associated patterns of behaviour and biological purpose.

He knew that the mountains of data he had collected represented an entirely new understanding of tidal resonance in photo-biology and its triggering effects upon patterns of evolution and mutation. The potential for determining optimum periods to create new forms was enormous. But now, laying out his discoveries no longer seemed important.

He needed to be with her.

He had wanted to fly out immediately but both the police and Dominique's production company counselled him to wait for Mitchell's return. He had pored over maps of the reserve. He started learning the local language. He prepared all the gear he would need. Still there was no news. A dull ache gnawed in the pit of his stomach. He listened to old tapes of natural effects that Dominique had recorded on previous trips. For days he listened to them; bird song, insect chirrup, the chattering of macaques; wave lap, the splatter of a tropical downpour. Occasionally, small snatches of her voice could be heard, fragments of dislocated sound, identifying specific effects. He looked through all his photos of her. It was the not knowing if she was alive or not that was the hardest to bear.

Eventually, Mitchell had flown back. His explanation of what had happened was sketchy. He had woken up one morning and Dominique wasn't there. Her recorder, microphones and day-kit were missing. He assumed she had gone off to make a recording of the dawn chorus. By the late afternoon she still hadn't returned.

Detectives had interviewed Mitchell. They had found no evidence to suggest that he was lying. Although they hadn't ruled out murder, Mitchell was not a suspect. There were several possibilities: Dominique had lost her way, or more likely, had got into some difficulty in the forest. She may have broken a leg and been unable to move. Their matter-of-fact tone altered only slightly as they told him she may have been eaten, perhaps by a crocodile or panther. They seemed to cheer up visibly as they told him it was more likely she had starved to death. Or she could have drowned in one of the rivers.

Frustrated by their seeming lack of genuine concern, it had been Villiers who had found himself proffering the suggestion that his wife may have been abducted, perhaps by poachers. They had looked at him quizzically. Or maybe terrorists ? Given the situation surely it was possible she may have been kidnapped by an extreme cell operating from some remote jungle base.

Their response seemed to turn to an ill-disguised pity, unhelpful, hardly reassuring. They thought it unlikely. Villiers had insisted on a further search-party. Together they had looked at the map. The reserve was vast. If someone who knew the area together with the local authorities couldn't find her, it was unlikely they would be able to help. Yes, they had uncovered foul play in some similar African cases but there was nothing to suggest that the local staff were anything but hard working and pious men. They would keep an open mind about the poacher theory but there really was nothing to suggest kidnapping. They were very sorry. In their opinion, it was doubtful that she was alive.

He had immediately finalised the arrangements for his own search and asked Mitchell to accompany him. He kept his eye on Mitchell. Since Dominique had disappeared the cameraman had visibly changed. His weather-beaten face had become drawn and gaunt, his eyes sinking further into their sockets. His gaze had become blank and withdrawn. A dark stubble grew like mould over his jaw. Villiers had occasionally found him alone and muttering, submerged in an inner world from which it was difficult to distract him. A question mark had begun to form in his mind about Mitchell's version of events.

* * *

The underside of the dinghy's bow scraped on the rocks below. They waded ashore and tied the boat to a clump of pandanus growing extravagantly along the water's edge.

Entering the undergrowth, Mitchell walked on ahead. They came to a dense thicket of *salak* and rattan palms. The *salak* stems were covered in long bony spines, but it was the rattan that you had to watch. Their overhanging fronds ended in a long whip-like tendril studded with sharp recurvent hooks. If they caught on your clothes, or as sometimes happened, in your nostril or ear, they pulled you to an immediate stop.

"It was about here," said Mitchell.

Villiers looked around him, trying to imagine the accident.

"The rattan caught her on the leg, she tripped and tumbled into the *salak* ..." His voice trailed off as he remembered.

Yes. There was definitely something veiled in Mitchell's tone. He went over the facts in his head as Mitchell had recounted them. Dominique's leg had been gashed by the rattan. By the time Mitchell had taken her boot off, her foot was already swelling. With Mitchell supporting her weight, they had hobbled down to the beach.

"What was funny ?" enquired Villiers, observing the camaraman's faint smile.

"Dominique. She let out such a stream of abuse as we limped down to the beach, swore at everything under the sun."

"Sounds like Dominique," he nodded. One minute she would pour out a torrent of invective, cursing the universe and all it contained, and the next minute she would be at her most vulnerable, crying uncontrollably as some memory from the nightmare of her childhood bubbled to the surface.

Mitchell was staring back at him. "By the time we got down to the water, Dominique was in tears …"

Villiers looked away. He sifted through the leaf-mould at his feet.

"Why ?" he heard himself saying.

"She was upset ... she felt that her childhood was effecting her marriage ... your marriage ... in a way she couldn't control."

"Dominique said this ?"

"Yes."

"What else ?"

"She was angry. She said she felt ... she described it as an inner compulsion ... to avenge herself for everything she'd suffered."

Villiers felt his head nodding involuntarily. The sounds of insects filled the gulf between them.

"She said she hated herself for hurting you ... but in a way she also needed to. She felt she was in a vicious circle. She wanted to change but felt powerless to do anything about it. And she hated that feeling of being powerless."

"Was there anything else ?" He could see Mitchell was trying not to smile.

"No."

Villiers looked out beyond the fringe of palms to the small patch of sea just visible through the gap. He could hear the sound of the waves on the beach.

"Do you think her injury had something to do with her disappearance ?"

"Her injury ? as a child you mean ?"

"I mean her leg."

"Ah, no, I don't think so. It was about four months between then and when she ... vanished."

The smile had gone. He wondered what else she had told him.

"Do you think Dominique's still alive, Mitchell ?"

"I ... I don't know."

Villiers nodded. "I found this," he said, passing Mitchell a sock, "just down there."

Mitchell took it and looked at it.

"It's Dominique's, isn't it ?"

"Yes." Mitchell handed it back to Villiers. Their gaze met, and for one curious instant Villiers felt as if he was looking into a mirror.

"Come on," he said, "let's go."

"We've only just got here."

"Dominique isn't here, Mitchell."

* * *

The boat chugged towards the mainland. Already the volcano was far behind them. A thin filament of moon hung like an eyelash low in the sky. Villiers felt the familiar boundaries of his experience disintegrating and collapsing within him. Powerful compulsions were wrestling inside as if they had a life of their own. An urgent adjustment seemed necessary. Yet through the conflicting turmoil, a new demand was quietly but insistently requesting his attention. If he could just hear it for long enough, this voice that seemed to whisper in his ear. It was her voice. It was definitely her voice. He had heard it so many times before. Yet now it sounded new, changed in some way. She was trying to tell him something but he had no idea what it was. He looked up at the sky, searching for the moon's crescent that had been there only moments before. It was gone, its pale sliver engulfed in the afternoon sun.

The contours of the mainland reserve were now becoming visible on the horizon. At last he had some intimation of the territory into which he was entering. He had come this far by a sheer exertion of will, but now, even if he could summon the conscious sustained effort, he knew that will alone could never pioneer the overgrown and neglected tracks of the jungle ahead.

The sky had noticeably darkened. He looked up to see the moon passing slowly in front of the sun. A large segment of the solar disk was already obscured. In the dim half-light, the eclipse gradually became more complete.

He could hear that voice calling him again. He was sure it was Dominique. Now, only a thin corolla of light glowed around the moon's black orb. There it was again. Far away, deep within him he heard it, as if the occultation had somehow increased his own receptivity. It was calling him by name …

"Villiers ... Villiers ..."

He trembled. His whole body was shaking.

"Villiers ... Villiers, for Christ's sake man, snap out of it !"

He felt Mitchell's enormous silhouette standing over him, gripping him by the arm.

"Don't look at it, Villiers, for Christ's sake, don't look at it ..."

He could hear Mitchell shouting as if from afar. He was unsure whether his eyes were open or closed. He reached up, touching them with his fingers. They were open; the bright annulus-shaped syzygy was now etched upon his brain, a golden white ring hovering before him. He closed his eyes, the after-image glowing deep within his brow.

* * *

The boat cruised up the channel towards the bay. As they had followed the coastline of the sanctuary along the isthmus, Villiers had begun to sense something of the pull which seemed to emanate from this region. Its low jungle-clad foothills exuded an undeniable allure, lifting like the mist from the epiphytic-festooned canopy. Now, with the western range rising before him, he felt he was beginning to understand the primal appeal this attraction must have had for Dominique. The contours of the primitive topography seemed to correspond with some ancient urge within, as if its compelling call, emerging through the geomorphic features of the landscape, correlated to a subjective yearning inside. He could well imagine Dominique's affinity to the place. Somewhere deep in the interior, that yearning would be satisfied. Towering over the foothills, the bluish shape of the western massif rose like a ship above the jungle. He was certain he would find her there, somewhere in that mountain range.

He took off his dark glasses and shook his head. Still the after-image of the sun's bright ring superimposed itself upon his vision. He wondered if perhaps he had permanently damaged his sight. Already he could see stars shining in the sky above. Surely they weren't always visible this early in the tropics ? He rubbed his eyes as they approached the shore and put the glasses back on. The stellar pattern refused to disappear.

The sun was starting to dip towards the western extremity of the bay as they dropped anchor in its shallow waters and rowed ashore. The boatman helped unload the supplies. They carried them along the sandy beach and up the short track to the watch-tower that would be their camp.

Vast clouds of fruit bats swarmed overhead, their leathery wings flapping loudly above the tree-tops. Flock after raucous flock lifted from their roosts and swooped low over the bay, heading towards the off-shore islands for their evening forage. Their penetrating screeches accented the growing hum of the nocturnal chorus. In the shifting half-light of rapid nightfall, erratic phrases of animal sound layered the incessant undertone of unseen insects.

By the time darkness had fallen they had finished bringing all the stores to the base of the tower. Nothing, however, could induce the boat-owner to stay the night.

"*Banyak binatang jahat*," he said. Too many evil animals.

Villiers marvelled at the strength of the seafarer's superstition. He would prefer the long unlit journey back to the harbour town over a single night in the jungle. Villiers paid him for their passage, thanking him prolifically, and wished him a safe return.

They watched the boat motor over the tranquil surface of the bay, slicing threads of silver in its wake. The thin lunar crescent, as if pursuing the sunset, stalked off into the sea. Its twin horns, poised on the horizon like an ark, looked for one transitory moment, as if it too might sail away, but then, with a sudden synodic plunge, it sank from sight beneath the sea.

They were alone.

It seemed like a good time to take stock of the situation, to gather in his mind some of the circumstances which had brought him to this shore. Mitchell too, seemed absorbed in his own reflections.

He looked around him. To the west, the Evening Star was now the brightest object in the night sky. At the western point of the bay, above the gentle incline of the cape, he could see the constellation of Orion, bright in the fading after-glow of the moon. The blue and white flashes of Rigel hovered on the horizon. Cocked at a provocative angle, the studs of the hunter's belt gleamed white and violet. There, on his right shoulder, was the alpha star, with its flickering orange light. His eyes finally drifted to the Great Nebula in Orion and remained focused there. Why, he wondered, did he feel such a peculiar schoolboy fascination for those glowing clouds of ionised gas ? Why did a mass of incandescent hydrogen, light years away from his own private world, hold such a sway over his attention ? As he gazed up at the fluorescing nebula, he sensed some nagging thought beginning to trouble the back of his mind, as if the mask or disguise of a particularly disagreeable horror was about to drop away. It felt like some disturbing ancestral taboo had dislodged itself from the pool of his memory and was trying to bubble to the surface.

He recalled the time when he was four, when his mother had found him rubbing himself as he lay face down on the bed. She had been washing her hair in the bathroom next door. She had stormed into the bedroom, her wet hair hanging in strands down her face and the towel flapping around her shoulders. She pulled off the sheets and grabbed him by the arm. He could still hear her words as if it were yesterday. 'If I catch you doing that just one more time, I'll cut it off. Do you hear me ? I'll cut it off with the carving knife.'

She had kept on shaking his arm.

'Understand ?'

No. He didn't understand.

She marched into the kitchen and came back with the carving knife.

'See this ?' she said, holding the gently curved blade up to her face. 'I'll cut it off with this.'

He had looked up and been unable to recognise her face. She wasn't usually like this.

He shuddered. It wasn't the first time the memory had flooded through him, yet none of the outrage had diminished. How much of his time since, he wondered, had been spent in trying to link back beyond that pivotal moment, when the image that he held of her had changed forever ? How much of his energy had been consumed in attempting to restore that original vision ? Were there still darker secrets, constellated in those maddingly ill-defined regions, other more hideous apparitions that lurked unsounded in the fathomless depths ? He sensed their existence but couldn't yet track them down.

Yet he knew that his ability to discern the changing patterns of psychic energy that linked him inextricably with Dominique was growing. She had experienced the most appalling circumstances in childhood, and he understood her reluctance to go back to investigate. With Dominique, it was as if the traumatic conditions in her past had propelled her forward, like the initial explosive event of an expanding cosmos, but the pain which she constantly sought to avoid, pursued her wherever she went. He wondered if the special conditions which seemed to exist here, in the nature reserve, had created an environment in which that momentum had somehow begun to slow, in which she had begun to feel it safe to stop and turn around. What exactly would she see, he wondered, as she glanced over her shoulder ?

The hum of the boat was growing faint in the distance. Its red and green navigation lights disappeared beyond the promontory to the north-east. His night vision continued to amaze him. He would never have believed that so many of the stars he knew could be visible here, away from the adulterating light of civilization. He looked behind him. The revolving lamp of the lighthouse at the western point spun its white arc around again. Just visible above the dark outline of land, where the highland slopes met the foothills, the bright stars of the Southern Cross hung low in the sky. He could see not just the familiar constellations, but thousands and thousands of the smaller suns and starry clusters which lay scattered along the adjoining spoke of the Milky Way.

He rubbed his eyes. It was a shock to discover he was still wearing his sunglasses. He took them off.

Mitchell, standing beside him, was watching him intently.

"You all right, Villiers ?" he asked.

For a moment he had been almost blinded, so bright was the cosmic panorama around him.

"I'm fine," he replied, "just adjusting to the light."

Mitchell stood there looking at him.

Behind Mitchell's shoulder, he could see the unmistakable shape of the Scorpion stretched out overhead, its pincers dipping towards the western horizon. The star Antares, red and green, glimmered turbulently on its thorax.

THE WATCHTOWER

He followed Villiers back along the beach. They turned up the track towards the watch-tower. The last of the fruit bats winged overhead. Large crabs scuttled back to the shelter of their burrows as they crunched along the coral path that bridged the mudflats.

They reached the base of the tower. The formidable array of supplies would all have to be hauled up the ladder and stored away. Villiers lit a hurricane lamp and climbed the steps to the hut, opening the trap-door built into its floor. He put a new mantle in a pressure lamp and hung it, hissing loudly, from one of the crossbeams. Within seconds, insects were swarming around the bright light; a large moth battering itself violently against the glass. They took the other lamp down below and started carrying the stores up through the hatch.

The hut was divided into three rooms. The largest, surrounded on three sides by open windows, looked out over a grassy stretch of wild pasture. All the stores they didn't immediately need, they put in one of the smaller rooms. The third room, the smallest, which looked like it would leak in the slightest rain, had a resident leaf-nosed bat dangling from one of the rafters. The bat, opening its reddish-brown eyes, watched them as they rearranged the equipment, but disinterested, was soon dozing again, swaying, ever so slightly, in the cool evening breeze. It didn't take as long as they had thought to bring all the stores up the ladder and stash them away.

Mitchell lit a mosquito coil. He watched the acrid smoke drifting away. They never did any good, these coils. A waste of money. He took out his foam mat and placed it on the floor. Above it he carefully hung his mosquito net. At last, he lay down on the mat and felt his body relax. In a strange way it was good to be back. He let the sides of the net drop to the floor and through its narrow mesh watched Villiers unpack his gear.

He remembered that day on the island. It was a complete disaster. Dominique had dragged him to the forest floor and within seconds was on top of him. The sharp spines and thorny vegetation beneath him had dug into his back and was so painful he thought he couldn't continue. At that point, he had looked up and once again seen the python, its belly unbelievably distended, digesting in the branch overhead. Dominique had got her leg caught on the rattan and to make matters worse, put her hand down on some *salak* spines. She screamed in agony and they'd had to call it off. When he got to his feet, he discovered his back was lacerated, raw and wet with blood. Together they had hobbled down to the beach, Mitchell taking the weight off Dominique's swelling ankle.

Dominique had lain on the shore, her feet paddling in the shallows. He helped pull the last of the spines from her foot and they had laughed at their futile efforts. Foam had frothed over her body, leaving little shorelines of salt drying on her skin. Between her legs, the pink bud of her sex opened as he watched. It seemed to Mitchell that some rare species of mollusc had cast off its shell and summoned by an irresistible law of nature, had swum from the dark caverns of the ocean floor to this beach, its ancestral breeding ground, during the one moon of the year on which it was possible to mate. She pulled him into her arms. The palm trees crackled in the heat of the equatorial noon. The sun beat down against his back. Her fingernails dug like claws into the exposed flesh on his shoulders. The salt stung his back to an intense numbness. Reddish brown clouds stained the sea around them, clots of blood dissolving in the foam.

It was the only time they had ever done it.

Somewhere in the distance, a night-bird let out a high rasping screech. Leaves rustled against the windows. Whenever the wind blew a little stronger, one of the branches rubbed noisily against the wallboards - an annoying grating sound that once noticed was hard to ignore or filter out.

On the other side of the hut Villiers was still trying to organise himself. God, look at him, trying to put up that mosquito net. Idiot. At last he sat down, took out his journal and started writing. What on earth had she ever seen in him?

Dominique. After two years of working together their sudden intimacy had genuinely surprised him. He had always been attracted to her. Her wild looks only magnified the natural magnetism which seemed to ooze out of her very being. But his hopes for their relationship had been immediately shattered. The sudden outbreaks of anger that had characterized their partnership while working immediately became more frequent; more violent, more disruptive. There was nothing at all attractive in this anger that Dominique hurled at him. It repelled him powerfully. It was as if some switch at her electro-magnetic core had reversed polarity.

For days on end they had fought and fought until it became almost impossible to work.

He remembered the occasion when some stray and innocuous remark of his had so offended her that she had picked up cans of film and threw them, like flying saucers, while he tried to duck in the corner of the tower. Spiced with abuse, they had flown all around him, bouncing off the walls until one finally hit him full in the face. A second later, another smashed one of the windows and sailed on through the trees to the pasture below. He had thought the sound of shattering glass might subdue her outburst. Instead it seemed only to add fuel to the fire. For one brief moment, he realised that she was deliberately trying to provoke him and on no account should he say or do anything. He felt himself withdrawing, as if melting into the wall of the hut, watching from a distance. She came towards him, lunged at him, and as if determined to drag him back into her arena, grabbed him by the hair, pulling away whole handfuls. Finally, when he had sat down again, she picked up one of the cans and ripped the camera-tape from its rim, pulling out the now exposed roll of film and dashing it to the floor. It was too much. He got up and walked to the trap-door. She screamed in his face as he passed. Saliva burned in the corners of his eyes. He scrambled down the ladder and walked off into the darkness of the jungle night.

He wasn't sure if she was in her sleeping bag when he returned later that night, but the next morning she was gone.

He looked over at Villiers. He had put down his journal and was mending the sock they had found that morning on the island.

"Where do we start ?" Villiers asked.

Your wife's mad and I fucked her, he wanted to say.

"The river systems. We'll explore the rivers and streams first. If Dominique is alive she can't be far from water."

"When we came in ... I had a feeling that Dominique might be in the highlands. Seemed like her kind of place."

"The whole reserve is her kind of place."

He watched as Villiers finished darning the sock and put his needle and thread away. He hung the sock on a line to dry and climbed back under his net.

A tokay gecko had started its loud throaty refrain in the trees outside.

"Goodnight, Mitchell."

"Yeah, sleep well."

THE PEACOCK'S TAIL

Sleep well. The sentiment echoed mockingly in his ear as he watched Mitchell turn out the pressure lamp. Its loud hissing died away to leave only the sounds of the night. As the light from the mantle slowly faded, a large moth flapped against the glass, its heavy thuds still audible long after the darkness had wrapped around them. Sleep well. Pleasant dreams.

The gecko's croak punctuated the unbroken hum of the night insects. Somewhere over on the other side of the pasture, the strident screech of a peafowl pierced the euphonic buzz. Far off in the distance, he could just make out the faint regular sigh of the sea, its waves breaking gently on the protected shore of the bay.

He closed his eyes. He felt his mind follow the constant chirrup along the coral track to a beach where a vast herd of whales had been washed up and were stranded on the sands. Why did they do this ? he heard himself wondering. Some of them were already dead; others were still alive. He and an unknown man were trying to get one of them back into the sea. They pushed and pushed but it wouldn't budge. He turned around and saw hundreds more stranded in the shallow waters of the bay. It was useless. The whales were dead or dying. There was nothing he could do. Flocks of seagulls were wheeling raucously above him. A mournful elongated sound, like nothing he had ever heard before, seemed to emanate from the head of the whale. Its eye grew white and opaque. The seagulls squawked all around, their wings flapping like so many umbrellas gone berserk. Cackling hideously, one of the gulls landed on the whale and started pecking at its eye. Again and again it dipped its bright yellow beak into the eye, extracting long strands of a jelly-like plasma. He turned to speak to the unknown man but he had gone. Slowly, with all the measured grace of a visiting dignitary, a peacock walked along the length of the whale's back. The gulls took off in an angry cloud as the peacock reached the whale's head. It turned towards him, and blinked, silently displaying the full fan of its iridescent tail.

Next morning, they bathed in the stream, had breakfast, and waited for the Conservation Department staff to arrive from their headquarters on the off-lying island. They should have checked in with them last night, but it had been late and Mitchell, who had scant regard for the interminable red-tape that surrounded even the most simple action here, had said to ignore them. They would motor over the narrow channel soon enough.

Villiers became enchanted with the large family of macaques that had moved in to check on the latest inhabitants of the hut. They swarmed over the roof and jumped noisily from the treetops, chattering excitedly, crashing through the leaves like amateurs. An old male scratched himself with vigour, his genitals dangling indecorously.

Villiers wandered out to the middle of the pasture where a herd of nervous banteng eyed him with curiosity, chewing solemnly on their cuds. Their doleful expressions gave way to alarm when the black bull got to its feet and bustled them off into the undergrowth, lowing discontentedly.

Several green jungle fowl fossicked in the margins of scrub along the pasture edge. As he turned back towards the watch-tower he saw two peafowl emerge from behind a large bush. He froze. He knew they were shy alert birds that usually took off at the first sign of human presence. Yet they seemed not to notice him. He was surprised how drab these wild birds were compared to the ones he had seen in parks back home. Perhaps it was already their moulting season ? He paused as the vivid images from the night before suddenly flooded through his mind. The straggly male in front of him was a pale reflection of the resplendent vision in his dream. He remembered its quivering crest, the glistening metallic blue, and the strange blink it had given as it had unfurled the jeweled ocelli of its tail.

He was still grappling with the images when he heard the sound of the boat approaching across the bay.

Mitchell was brewing another cup of coffee when he returned to the tower. The head warden soon arrived with two guards. From what Mitchell had been saying, Villiers had been expecting an unpleasant and officious pedant. Instead he found the warden a charming man, with a wry wit, a generous nature and a detailed knowledge of the reserve and its wildlife. After the permissions had been checked and the required fee changed hands they settled down to enjoy the coffee. They were surprised and delighted that Villiers knew enough of their language to converse quite freely.

"No," the warden said, "nobody had seen Dominique."

He was embarrassed to discover a tear forming in the corner of his eye.

"But two zoology students …" continued the warden as he unfolded his map, "… they were studying the reproductive cycle of the green turtle … they saw footprints on one of the western beaches. Just here …"

Villiers noted the position of the beach on the map.

"How long ago ?"

"About six weeks, maybe more."

"Are the students still here ?" he asked.

"They went back last week."

Villiers bit his lip.

"Was there anybody else in the area ? Poachers ?"

The warden looked incensed. "There aren't any poachers here," he said, "except these two." He pointed to the two guards. They were both former poachers. Jamad, the eldest, had an earthy sense of humour and a piratical expression. He was soon pricing everything in sight and converting it to the local currency.

Villiers watched his face as he made the mental

calculations. He imagined how much rice Jamad could buy for his young wife and new-born child with the cash equivalent of even their most simple piece of equipment. He took an instant shine to him.

They arranged for Jamad to return the following day to accompany them on their first foray into the interior. As the three men got up to leave, Villiers noticed the distinct coolness between them and Mitchell.

After they had left Mitchell looked thoughtful. "No poachers ?" he snarled. "Don't you believe it. It's too lucrative for them to ever eradicate. What we can't be sure of is how much they're in on it."

"It could be Dominique."

"Poachers. Or nest-gatherers," argued Mitchell. "There's caves on that coast full of swifts. The villagers sneak in whenever they can ... they sell the nests for soup."

"You don't think it's worth checking there first?" he asked.

"No. I think we should check the river systems first. She'll stay close to water."

"But aren't there streams in the mountains ? We could check them."

Mitchell looked at him, his gaze narrowing

slightly. "I think we should check the river systems first," he repeated.

Villiers stood up. "I'm going for a swim. Coming?"

"I'll stay here and tidy up. See you later."

Villiers took his diving mask and towel and walked down the track to the beach. He knew that if they found Dominique it would be through a combination of luck, intuition and sheer physical exertion. But it was Mitchell who knew the park. For the time being he would have to go along with Mitchell's plans.

He walked out onto the beach. He was relieved to see there weren't any whales washed up on the shore. The sand scorched the soles of his feet. He took off his clothes and ran down to the water. Putting his mask on, he lowered himself beneath the surface, the tension of their rivalry instantly washing away.

He swam further out and dived down amongst the shoals of fish that were casually grazing on seaweed at the bottom. They were totally indifferent to his presence. He stroked out further, past the muffled outline of a stingray hidden beneath the sand. Years of diving had increased his capacity to hold his breath. He enjoyed seeing how long he could stay underwater, how far down he could dive, pushing himself to his limit, and if he could, a little beyond. He swam along a ridge of coral, savouring the last of his air. Small fish swam in and out of the weeds, shifting in the current. Below him, dotted here and there, sea urchins nestled on ledges in the rock. He pushed down deeper, into a narrow canyon between two ridges. This was the moment he enjoyed, stretched between breaths, suspended weightless, his whole body humming. The underwater sounds throbbed in his eardrums as he stroked upwards. In a graceful parabolic curve he rose through the softly diffused layers of light, a thin stream of bubbles trailing from his nostrils. Breaking the surface, he regulated the flow of air in a long controlled inhalation, once again feeling his lungs expand.

He floated on his back, the bright blue vault of the sky arched far above him. A white egret flew across his field of vision. As he swam slowly back to shore he noticed a large dark shape making its way through the water towards the mouth of the estuary. It was only by diving underwater that he was able to recognise the sleek belly of a monitor lizard, mottled yellow, green and grey; its short legs paddling comically while the powerful movements of its tail propelled it forward. The lizard passed beyond the shallow bar of sand where the fresh water met the sea and kept on swimming upstream. Villiers followed it.

Large *nipa* palms grew straight out from the water. Villiers wondered how they survived such extreme salinity. Their seed pods, shaped like the armoured mace on the end of a dinosaur's tail, protruded menacingly from between their fronds.

A sense of claustrophobic fear crept through him as he made his way up the murky waters of the narrowing stream. Its overhanging branches and muddy banks, so different from the open reaches of the bay he had just left, filled him with a horror of unseen menace, a danger lurking below. His toes squelched unpleasantly in the mud on the bottom. He had a dread of stepping on something soft or moving.

He was just considering whether to return or not when the monitor climbed out of the water onto a narrow shingle beach. Only then did Villiers see how large it was - over seven feet long. It tasted the air cautiously with its forked tongue, so similar to a snake's except much larger. Evidently satisfied that it was alone, it moved up the beach to an overhanging bank where a clutter of decomposing debris had been washed ashore.

Villiers decided that as long as he remained beneath the surface the lizard could neither see nor smell him.

The monitor started scratching amongst the gravel and earth with its hind legs. Soon it had scraped out a sizeable hole. Villiers watched in amazement as the first egg popped out and dropped into the nest. One after another they came, a production line of gleaming oblate spheres. Carefully edging closer, he could see the abdominal muscles contracting and then expanding as each soft-shelled ovoid emerged from the lizard's protrusive vulvar opening.

He had become so absorbed in the egg-laying process that when he again turned to look at the lizard's head, he was startled to realise he'd been seen. The monitor looked back at him, steadily returning his gaze. Its long tongue flicked in and out. Villiers saw that - whatever danger he might represent to it - the lizard had been interrupted midway in a physiological process over which it no longer had any control. It had no choice. It could only continue laying. Another parchment-skinned egg fell from its cloacal opening. In the stillness which encompassed them, gravid with natural sound, a new understanding began to crystallize in Villiers' mind.

Its last egg deposited, the monitor started to scrape sand and leaf-litter over its unborn clutch. Villiers ducked below the surface and swam back towards the beach to collect his clothes.

THE PANTHER'S CAVE

She could feel them getting closer. For days, she had been able to discern the eddies of their minds within the deep silence of the cave. Now as they approached, she could feel these two currents growing stronger; the one obsessed and dangerous, the other so irritatingly reasonable. Neither of them had responded to her signals.

The panther woke up with a start and licked itself under the chin. The parasite that had interrupted its dreams was soon despatched. Pausing now and then, it continued to wash in a more relaxed manner, moistening its coat to a glistening sheen.

Dominique watched the cat's elegant movements from her ledge above. She had covered its surface in layers of *alang-alang* grass, renewing them periodically as they became compacted. It had proved an extremely comfortable bed and the dry hay-like aromas that suffused through it when she nestled into its warmth were reassuring. She hadn't slept so well in her entire life.

The panther finished grooming itself and turned to look at her. Its nonchalant stare was punctuated with a blink. It blinked again. She knew what it would do next. Every day for the last three months, its routine had been unchanging. Yawning, it languorously stretched its haunches high into the air, its fore-paws gripping the uneven ground. With a careful leap, it dropped to the soft earth below and padded towards the cave-mouth. She watched as it paused at the entrance; it looked cautiously in both directions before venturing out into the late afternoon. The cat's rapid transformation from recumbent insouciance to huntress always amazed her.

She reached into the straw and pulled out a length of *salak* heart that she had cut the day before. She was finding it increasingly difficult to gather the sweet stalks. The walk to the palm grove, although not far, required climbing down several escarpments of slippery rock. Below - on a narrow flat on each side of a small stream - stood the thicket of *salak*. She had already exhausted the supply of young shoots from closer individual palms, and now even the grove itself was becoming depleted. And to get at the young growth, she had first to strip it of its long spines. The effort involved was exhausting, but now that the *salak* fruits were also ready, she had a large larder of instantly edible provisions. She had filled her entire kit the day before with stalk-lengths and the strange pangolin-skinned fruit. Together with nettles, the ever-plentiful coconuts, *nibung* nuts, several wild papayas and some small berries, her food-store would last for some time. Even the bananas in her garden were starting to ripen. She hoped they would be different from the others she had come across in the reserve - mealy and totally inedible. Dominique peeled the thin brown skin from one of the *salaks* and bit into the hard crunchy fruit. The sharp sour tang was a luxury after months of palm-heart and sago and the shell-fish she dug at low tide.

It would be several hours before the panther returned. Its devotion to her was complete. Some feline intuition must have been at work that day it found her by the stream. Instinctively, she had sought the higher ground of the mountainous region to the west, hiding below the undergrowth as the helicopter had flown overhead. But after weeks of hunger and exhaustion she had finally collapsed at the foot of a small waterfall, unable to go any further. She had filled her stomach with its reviving water and fallen asleep with its cool spray splashing against her face. It was the touch of the cat's rough tongue against her cheek that had awoken her.

Its black muzzle and pungent breath had, like a powerful mnemonic, catalysed a torrent of images through her mind. Almost immediately, the terror had propelled her into a dark oblivion.

For one brief moment she must have regained consciousness, for as the panther dragged her by the scruff of her fatigues, she remembered seeing the carcass of a cub lying amongst the leaves. The cat had put her down and gone over to her cub. The last thing she could remember seeing was the panther - its front claws firmly gripping the corpse of its young. It ate with a slow deliberation, licking it in mournful farewell. This strange act of cannibalism, like a ritual animistic consummation, seemed one of the most tender sights she had ever witnessed, a grieving mother's last act for her departed progeny. Unable to move, she waited her turn, convinced she would be next.

It had been the sound of Mitchell's voice which

had awoken her.

Unsure if she was still alive, she had heard his calls in the distance. The soft purrs of the cat beside her had stopped and it gave a low growl as his voice got closer.

"Dominique ... Dominique ..."

She had lain back on the slab of rock and gazed up at the roof of the cavern. A small colony of swifts had made their home there, safe from the attention of the cat. She had strained against the weight of her exhaustion to hear. All around her, water dripped from the icicle-like tips of stalactites. She listened to the approaching voice, unable to associate any meaning to the constantly repeated refrain.

"Dominique ... Dominique ..."

His voice echoed around the cavern, like a strange exotic cuckoo amongst the squeaking of the swifts. Through the clouded veils of her coma, it sounded like that of her father, angry and strident, demanding she come out of hiding. Why should she ? Why should she come out ? She knew he would hurt her again. She trembled with terror. He would pretend to be her friend. He would hold out some sweet for her, coaxing her forward until she was beside him at last.

Then he would snatch the sweet away, grab her by the arm, twisting it sharply behind her back, and beat her and beat her until she promised not to tell ...

Shaking uncontrollably, she rolled over into the soft warmth of the cat's dark fur. Hot wet tears ran down her cheeks as she burrowed into its velvety comfort.

The beam of the flashlight bounced over the walls towards her. She heard the panther's growl rise to the intruder.

"Dominique ?"

She nuzzled into the gratifying prominences on the cat's swollen belly and felt the warm rich milk obliterate the taste of her tears. She imagined with a smile the look of horror on her father's face as he stared into the snarling blue irises of the panther's eyes.

THE RIVER SYSTEM

Mitchell pushed the narrow *prahu* out from the bank and clambered into the stern. Jamad, sitting in the middle section, turned around to make sure he was safely onboard. Villiers crouched in the bow. They started paddling. The boat moved easily upstream. Although swollen with the rainy season floods, the river flowed with an unhurried lethargy. Mitchell watched as the last of the pasture lands glided by. A bull banteng looked up at them as they passed. It swished its tail, as if directing river traffic, and then, satisfied that its orders had been obeyed, resumed grazing. A heron lifted gracefully from the river and lofted away above the trees. Here and there *nipa* palms thrust defiantly out of the mud, their seedpods raised like weapons of menace. Mitchell stared at the back of Villiers' head as they paddled.

Already they were deep in the forest. A kingfisher, bright green and blue, saw them as they rounded a bend in the river, and darting off its perch, disappeared upstream. The river narrowed. Walls of green surrounded them. A dense confusion of palms and strangler-vines grew down to the edge of the embankment. They paddled on, pushing through the overhanging fronds. The canopy spread over the still dark water, shutting out the sky. A tunnel of foliage stretched out before them. Fallen forest giants lay rotting on the river-bank. The dank decomposing odours of vegetation and mud hung like a fecund mist above the water. Every time Mitchell had explored one of these rivers he felt he was travelling back in time to some primeval pre-dawn, to a world in which evolutionary experiment flourished in humid proliferation.

He looked down at the black mirror below him, his inky reflection whirling around the eddies of his paddle. A vortex of memories opened up within, surging through him in a vivid synaptic flood. Her hair ... he would never forget that evening he had found her lying face down in the earth. He had no idea how long she'd been there. As he bent down towards her, he had discovered two slugs, spotted like leopards, mating in her hair. Fallen from the underbrush, they coiled around each other, entwined in her dark curls, exuding a thick pearly mucus that bubbled and foamed in a soapy opalescence. They revolved around and around in a slow spiral dance, as if intending to unravel the secrets of her dreams. As he looked closer, he saw the enormous antler-like penile protrusions with which they clasped each other. He thought about filming them and was just starting to wonder if it was a practical possibility when she had woken up, frowned at his close proximity and stalked off back to the hut, the amorous gastropods still clinging to her flowing locks.

His paddle slid again beneath the surface, disturbing the decomposing vegetation that lay on the riverbed. With each stroke it seemed he was gliding further down the riverine passages of his mind, into some umbral region where rapidly multiplying images, all roaring for attention, jostled and swirled along the ever-receding tributaries.

They had stood at the top of the waterfall and looked down. Dominique stared at the cascade below them as if in deep trance. A hundred feet below, the water smashed against the rocks in a thunderous white spray. Mitchell peered into the mist. The faint prismatic veil of a rainbow shone in the moist air. A formation of parakeets, lime green with yellow and red heads, winged through the spray - a cool midday shower in the tropical heat. He looked up at Dominique. She had sat down on one of the rocks, and begun to sway in a gently rhythmic motion, lost in a world of her own. That vision of her, rocking back and forth, like the pendulum of a giant invisible clock, remained indelibly in his mind. She hugged her knees, gradually gathering momentum like the disturbed movement of some hypomanic metronome. He went over to where she sat. She reached into her jacket and pulled out the canister of lithium. 'I won't be needing these anymore,' she'd said, a conspiratorial gleam in her eye. She stood up and tossed the canister into the stream. The prescription bobbed to the surface and shot over the edge. They watched as it transcribed a graceful arc then disappeared into the spray.

Mitchell's paddle struck rock. He looked up. They had reached the travertine terraces in the upper reaches of the river. They got out of the *prahu*, hauled it up the terraced steps, and once again clambered in and pushed off. Within minutes the steady sibilance of the water-chutes was behind them, lost in an eerie blanket of sparse jungle sound.

A large hornbill, disturbed from its arboreal roost, flapped noisily overhead, its long beak and clumsy flight giving it the appearance of a nose-heavy fighter biplane, returning from one mission too many.

They paddled on. A troop of black langurs caught his attention in the upper canopy, their haunting drawn-out calls echoing within him as they dashed off through the tree tops.

It was a similar sound he had heard one night as he awoke from his sleep in the watchtower. He had followed it down the coral path to the beach and found Dominique, lying in the shallows, wailing in the dark. The unearthly sound carried out across the bay like an ancient invocation, charged with generations of power. Her body had shone like polished moonstone. He sat down and watched as she rolled about in the wavelets. Clutching handfuls of wet sand, she rubbed them over her body, coating herself in a glistening silicaceous skin. Phosphorescent plankton glowed in the sand, their pulverised cells releasing a shining bioluminescent jelly, fluorescing like a veil of miniature flash-guns. He watched as she lay there like some photo-electric mermaid, inviting the mariners of her mind to an elaborate aquatic orgy.

It was some time before she stood up and waded out into the bay, diving into its warm waters to leave him alone with his thoughts. The moon had set. He grew cold sitting in the sand, wondering if he should follow her. At last, she had emerged and walked, like some amphibious sleepwalker, up the beach to the hut.

Jamad suddenly signalled them to stop paddling.

"*Badak*," he whispered.

Mitchell craned forward but could see nothing. Jamad tapped the end of his nose and sniffed. The smell, like fresh horse manure, was so strong Mitchell couldn't understand why he hadn't noticed it before. Villiers crouched lower in the bow. Only Jamad paddled, manoeuvring the *prahu* silently through the water.

They turned a bend. Half-submerged in the muddy water by the far riverbank, the rhino basked oblivious of their arrival. It sank deeper into the mud, only its grey snout and stubby little horn visible above the surface. Every so often its ear twitched, thrashing the water like a propeller.

No fucking camera, thought Mitchell. Watching

the world's rarest large land mammal and no camera. Even his stills was packed away.

A loud snort from the riverbank announced the presence of another rhino hidden in the thick vegetation. It crashed through the branches and emerged abruptly from the undergrowth. It was obviously a male.

As quietly as he could, Mitchell undid the straps on his pack and ferreted around for his camera-case.

The female clambered noisily from the river, water streaming down the folds of its armour-like skin, and climbed up the riverbank to a clearing where the churned mud suggested years of use.

The male marched towards her, snorting vigourously. The female turned its rump towards him. Pissing a violet stream all over the wallow, the male sniffed her with rampant enthusiasm.

Surely they weren't going to ... no, he couldn't believe it ... The male rhinoceros, without any further preliminaries, lifted his feet onto the female's back and mounted her.

He was witnessing something that he thought he'd never see. This was the very image he had hunted for so long, the very reason he had first come to the reserve. No one had ever filmed this. To the best of his knowledge no one had even seen it before. He looked on in impotent rage, his fingers fumbling with the camera-case, his vision blurred with frustration. Over and over, the thought kept hammering away in his mind, obscuring the scene before him; this was something he'd never see again.

"C'mon," said Villiers, his voice loud with impatience, "I haven't come all this way to see animals fucking. Let's go."

The rhinos bellowed in confusion and crashed off into the jungle, snorting loudly. The sound of breaking branches continued for some time into the distance.

"C'mon" repeated Villiers, turning around, "we're here for a reason."

Mitchell felt his anger concentrate and narrow as he returned Villiers' gaze. Their eyes locked. He was surprised to see how fierce Villiers looked. He gazed down at his camera. A cool calm swept through him. The metallic hum of insects surged into the stillness. I could kill you, quite easily, he thought.

THE NIGHT FIRES

Villiers stared into the fire. Its resinous wood burnt with a fierce intensity. The flames crackled orange and violet, cradling the twisted and blackened branches. A twig snapped and flew off into the darkness. He looked up and saw Mitchell trimming his nails with an army knife.

Looking at those rhino today, he had imagined them together and his anger had boiled over. He knew Mitchell, given half a chance, would never say no. It wasn't the duplicity; the betrayal, that upset him. What tore at the very centre of his existence was the possibility of sheer futility, a sense of wasted time that cut against the grain of every thought and belief he valued. For years he had nurtured a long patient process with Dominique, believing in the peculiar magic of their meeting. It had been at a time when both of them had ached to end the isolation they experienced. They had both sent out messages, loud and heartfelt, a kind of psychic SOS. When their eyes had first met, he was sure those messages had been answered.

He often marvelled at the series of odd coincidences that had brought them together, and the way in which, despite their seemingly unresolvable problems, his sense of discovery had grown. Dominique's uncanny ability to foresee events had so surprised him that it took him some time to realise that her premonitions, invariably accurate, were won at great cost. Her gift seemed so effortless that at first he hadn't noticed how, after each time she submerged herself into that special state of relaxed concentration from which her visions sprang, a corresponding descent into violent unpredictability would unerringly follow. It was as if there was a part of her which continually needed to renew itself and could do so only by extremes of self-destruction. Somehow, that wild mix of prophetic certainty and childlike vulnerability had aroused in him an instinct more maternal than he could ever explain.

It was in the intervals of calm that she saw her visions. But never far away there was always that dark cocktail of raw unbridled aggression and irrational argument, coupled with an absolute and unassailable certainty of her own lack of blame. Such episodes flared up without warning again and again and within moments got out of hand. They were followed, eventually, by a truly extraordinary ability to selectively forget, as if each new day was unconnected to the last by anything so inconvenient or unsettling as memory.

He remembered their last few weeks together. Irrational arguments had followed one on top of another. Nothing he did could please her. Then, on the night before she had left, they had made love. It was the first time in over a year.

A mosquito buzzed around his ears. He watched as Mitchell got up and walked off into the bushes. His night vision hadn't left him. Already he was growing accustomed to its spectral colours. He followed Mitchell's stooping gait through the undergrowth until it merged into the darkness.

How little it took, he thought, for lives to be uprooted, for directions to be so drastically altered. Desire. Grief. Whole lives fragmented and blasted off course.

Villiers looked up at the night sky. He remembered when he and his brother were in their teens and had gone on a camping trip. They lay on a beach in their sleeping bags, gazing into the night. His brother broke the silence, 'Look up at the stars,' he said, 'and feel your insignificance. We are nothing but ants in a vast galaxy, spinning through the cold reaches of space. Whole suns are born and burn and burn out and die. What does the universe care for human existence ? It's a universe of supreme indifference, cruel and savage, grinding all creatures before it in a remorseless struggle for survival. And survival for what ? The entire universe ... evolving only to inescapable extinction, a meaningless cycle of reproduction and death.'

He had felt a series of chill shivers run through him as he heard those words. He listened to the waves beating upon the shore. One after another they came, a regular rhythm, every ninth wave louder than the rest. He sat up and looked out to sea. The tide had come in. The waves glowed with phosphorescence. The horizon blurred. The stars swam before his eyes. Looking up, he saw the collapsing, condensing clouds of stellar dust in Orion's sword. He felt a moistening in the corner of his eye. 'No,' he replied, after what seemed like an age, 'you and I are flesh and blood; we are connected by invisible bonds. What you and I do effects the other. That's how it is. We are points of light in an ocean of pulsing energy. Waves move across its surface, currents swirl in its depths, tides shift its entire volume. Everything is interconnected. Who knows what effect even our most secret thought may have ? The universe is like a mirror, it reflects what's placed in front of it.' He lay back and felt as if he was stretched out across deep space, encompassing vast distances, arms outspread, looking down on the stars as he sped by. When he rolled over, he saw his brother was fast asleep.

They had returned from their holiday the next day and found lines of cars parked outside the house. They were the cars of relatives and family friends. A dreadful sinking awareness overtook him as they pulled up. He got out of the car as if in some horrible slowed-down nightmare and went inside. Half-familiar faces were all around him, their eyes mouthing mute condolence. He couldn't recall much of what happened after that. All he could remember was his father taking him by the hand into the bedroom, to tell him what he already knew. She had drowned. His mother had drowned.

Mitchell returned through the bushes. He adjusted his trousers and sat down beside the fire. Villiers turned and looked at him.

"More coffee ?"

"Sure."

Mitchell passed over his mug. Villiers poured the dark Javan brew, filling it to the brim. He passed it back.

"Thanks," said Mitchell.

Villiers caught his eye.

"Mitchell ?"

"Yeah ?"

"Did you ever sleep with Dominique ?"

He watched Mitchell's face assume a new mask.

"No."

"I just wondered."

Villiers sipped his coffee. The fire crackled softly between them. Sleeping in the tent nearby, Jamad gave a low moan, rolled over and was quiet once again. Mitchell cleared his throat. He spat a spray of coffee grinds into the flames. They hissed and spluttered, smouldering in an orange glow.

"The night before Dominique disappeared ... she told me something ..."

Villiers watched him carefully.

"She said ... she had demons."

"We all have demons, Mitchell."

"She said she was going to leave you. She had grown tired of you ... the way you questioned everything she did. You had become for her a kind of authority figure. She found herself loathing you."

"Anything else ?"

"She said leaving you was the only way she could understand what was inside her."

It was becoming increasingly difficult to tell when Mitchell was lying.

"Perhaps."

"Listen, she hated you, she'd had enough."

Villiers felt the animosity in the cameraman's voice.

"You listen to me," he said quietly, "What you know about her amounts to nothing. Got that ? Nothing."

"I know she wanted out."

"You still don't understand, do you ?"

Mitchell stared at him blankly.

"Understand what ?"

Villiers looked at the cameraman. This was a man so lost in the gloom of his own shadow that he could see nothing but darkness. No wonder he needed lenses to help him organise what stared him in the face.

"Why Dominique disappeared," replied Villiers.

Mitchell's face tightened into a half-squinting grimace.

"Tell me," he said.

Villiers felt a sudden reluctance to share the privacy of the messages he had received over the last few days. It occurred to him that if his hunch was correct, then Mitchell probably already knew. He looked into Mitchell's cold leaden eyes.

"Some other time," he said.

THE WILD DOGS

Mitchell walked slowly out into the clearing, signalling to the others to follow. A small herd of rusa, unaware of the intrusion, were browsing at the edge of the forest, chewing thoughtfully on clumps of sedge and the overhanging leaves of a large fig tree.

Jamad and Villiers moved up quietly behind him. Crouching down beside the rotting remains of a fallen log, they peered over at the herd. The stag sat in the shade, quietly ruminating, every once in a while scratching its flanks with the tines of its antlers. The rutting season over, its dark shaggy mane hung from its neck in long half-moulted tatters.

The afternoon light was fading and that golden magic hour, perfect for filming, had already begun. Once again he found himself cursing his lack of equipment.

Instinctively he put his binoculars to his eyes. As he watched, it became apparent that the entire herd of deer was being plagued by vast swarms of flies. They buzzed continuously around the heads and tails of the rusa, searching for a soft moist place in which to lay their eggs. The herd, determined to continue their forage, were becoming more and more distracted by the immense dark clouds that whirred around them. Their tails almost constantly whisked from side to side and their ears flapped violently. There was no respite. The flies were landing in their nostrils, their mouths, their eyes, any mucus membrane they could find, intent on giving their larvae a good start in life.

Putting its head up against the trunk of the tree the old stag began to rub itself rhythmically on the bark, crushing its tormentors. But looking through the binoculars, Mitchell could see its dark lips and nostrils were encrusted in a seething mass of flies.

The rest of the herd were doing no better. Shaking its head and madly flapping its ears, one young hind began to spin around and around in a tight circle, like a kitten chasing its tail. Another doe, visibly pregnant from an early-season mating, started to jump about like a demented gazelle then threw itself to the ground, again and again banging its head against the pasture, rubbing its neck and rear against a clump of sedge, repeatedly flicking its tail. As it writhed around on the grass Mitchell felt a curious space open up in his memory and the images of Dominique, her body covered in volcanic ash, began, in wildly disjointed fragments, to superimpose upon what he saw before him.

He held the field glasses tighter to his eyes, compelled to look, as if he had discovered some new unknown species and mindful that even a small peripheral distraction might interrupt the strange sequence of rapidly dissolving images. It was at that moment he heard the unmistakable *kee, kee, kee* - the peculiar high pitched barking of an adjag calling to the rest of its pack.

Instantly the stag snorted an alarm, but preoccupied with the bot-flies, the deer seemed slow to realise what was happening. Several took off into the tree-cover but within seconds the wild dogs, with a tremendous yapping, burst through the foliage, completely surprising the rest of the herd. One of the deer, getting to its feet, looked around only to see the lead dog leaping towards it. Paralysed by fear, it stood there, frozen to the spot as the dog, jaws open, lunged at it, grabbing it by the snout. The deer shook its head, wildly flailing from side to side as the dog, gripping with its teeth, hung on. Already it was eating the rusa's tongue. Another adjag ran up, fastening itself to the deer's hindquarters, and another, a huge yellowish-brown dog, sprang out of the forest and began snapping at the doe's soft underbelly.

Unsteady on its feet but still standing, the deer braced itself as they came out of the shadows, one after another, barking and yelping. One dog clamped itself to the doe's ear and another fastened onto its neck. Together with the lead dog they yanked and pulled and tugged until it tumbled over. Panting heavily, their tongues lolling from their jowls, the dogs sat on it, pinning it down while the rest of the pack joined them and immediately began to eat.

His eyes seemed glued to the binoculars. Again he felt a peculiar surge of energy as if the violently kicking doe had become a strange psychic window, a sluice-gate through which the memories of the past were flooding, one after another. And there was an older layer, one in all his years of filming he had never twigged to, an image so at the core of his being that now he could see the connection it didn't surprise him at all. He realised it was the memory of his mother and the particular circumstances of her death that, unconsciously, had drawn him towards becoming a wildlife cameraman. In the many detached moments of violent death he had filmed, witnessing but powerless to intervene, he was recreating a likeness, a replica, a parallel frame, of those brief seconds that had etched themselves on his brain forever. He suspected the knowledge of this link should in some way set him free but instead he felt perversely bound, entrapped, no closer to seeing a way forward beyond the disturbing mesh of fate that his life had become.

He turned around, for once feeling a strong affinity with Villiers, but he had gone. His boot-prints, together with Jamad's, lead like an arrow, back into the jungle.

THE OBSIDIAN BLADE

Men. What did they know about feminine mysteries ? They could dare only a timid trespass into a woman's domain. Grey shadowy ciphers, they lived like pond skimmers on the surface of life, thralls to technology, ignorant of the gifts within them.

Dominique got up from the fire and walked to the entrance of the cave. The moon's silver sickle hung above the horizon. A warm moist wind blew in from the bay, sweeping along the valley and up the cliff-face. It swirled through her hair and funnelled into the cave-mouth, where it circled like a captured whirl-wind, whistling around the cavern, vibrating the glistening stalactites to a loud resonant hum. The cave's entrance, like some natural sound-shell, broadcast the wind's high-pitched harmonics back into the night. One after another, hundreds of pale nest-building swifts flew from the cave-mouth in long string-like lines, pursuing the sonic frequencies as if chasing the nocturnal stridulations of some new untasted insect. She walked to the edge of the valley and looked down. In the pale lunar light, an ocean of palms rolled below her, their fronds rippling in the breeze. Echoing across from the far ridge, she could hear the faint note of a distant antiphonal response as it bounced down the hills and out to sea. Near perfect conditions, she thought. She turned back to the cave and walked inside.

She set up the mics, unpacked another reel of tape and laced it through the recorder. Putting on her headphones, she adjusted the levels and altered the bass/treble balance. She switched on. Through the headset the high plangent whistle spiralled in stereophonic orbit. One by one, the stalactites, dripping like calcareous teeth from the cave roof, sprung into Orphean life, like tuning forks in the mouth of some sleeping giant. The large white folds of limestone, cascading like drapery down the walls of the cave, joined in the chorus, wrapping the upper registers in a rich tonal embrace. On the far side of the cavern, an organ-piped stalagmite finally reached resonance, thrumming a low monophonic drone. All around her, gleaming pools of calcite crystals trilled on the threshold of human hearing. The flutter of wings continued as the swifts took to the air; their occasional squeak peppering the phase-locked frequencies.

Dominique removed the earphones and placed them on a rock. She walked over to the fire and fed more branches to the embers. Their dry limbs ignited instantly, flickering the cave walls with orange light. The wind blew trails of sparks high into the darkness above her. For a long time she gazed at the leaping tongues of flame.

I must prepare myself, she thought. She looked at the three half-crocks of coconut shell beside her, each one filled with a different colour; black from the soot of the fire, white and red from the coloured clays she had found along the riverbank. They rested on top of an enormous mound of silver-sand she'd carried up from the riverbed, laboriously hauling each load in the double shell of a coco-de-mer found on the shoreline. At its base sat a large conch, filled to the brim with fresh water. To the left, in another half-shell, a pomade of coconut oil and herbs clarified slowly in the heat. In front of her, cupped in the skin-like basal fold of a palm frond, was her mirror. Beside it glimmered the flake of obsidian she had picked up on the volcano, its black vitreous facets glinting in the firelight. Everything is ready, she thought.

She leant down and ran her fingers over the blade, feeling its glossy sharpness, reconnecting once again to the surge of energy she felt whenever she remembered the soft warm slopes of Krakatau and how they had shuddered beneath her. She could never forget how it had all become so strikingly clear, how she saw just exactly what she had to do, as if the volcano had blown away - once and for all - the last remaining obstructions that had kept her dormant for so long.

She stood up and stretched. The wind had changed direction and the last high-pitched harmonics, hovering on the edge of audibility, faded into the shadows. She looked down at the recorder. It was about to run out. The red tag on the end of the tape slid free across the record-head. The reel spun around noisily. She switched it off.

She walked along the narrow passageway to the entrance and stood, framed in its yawning arch, like some sacred figurine emerging from the portico of her feline parthenon, summoned by the tides to perform the all-important rites of empowerment. The lunar crescent edged closer to the sea. Out in the bay, white-water broke against the reef and swirled through the gaps in the rock. The foaming white waves, diminished by the natural barrier, curved across the shallow lagoon, streaming towards the beach. She watched them for a while, then set off along the narrow track, following the curve of the hill; the sheer drop to the sea on one side, the dark jungle on the other.

The sound of the water-chutes leaped out to greet her. She turned the last corner and walked past a thicket of flowering bamboo out to the rocks in the middle of the stream. Above and below her, small cascades tumbled through the overhanging ferns and splashed into a series of deep pools, dazzling like quicksilver in the moonlight. This was where she must bathe. She threw off her clothes and slipped into the cool refreshing water. She looked up at the waterfall. A carpet of green moss crept down the rockface, while all around her clumps of large-leaved epiphytes hung like spiders from the overhead branches. She lay there, suspended weightless, gazing through the ferns' feathered silhouettes as the moon descended slowly to the ocean's bright reflecting rim. As it sank beneath the horizon she felt a sharp tug within her, as once again the child changed position. She looked down at the large dome of her belly. The child, as if activated by the moon's sudden dip, wriggled restlessly, sending ripples of silver across the pool. She closed her eyes and sank below the surface, her hair swirling like pond-reeds in the current. It must be done, she thought.

She pulled herself up from the rock ledge. This was the moment she hated - adjusting once again to the tiresome pull of the earth's gravity. She felt so heavy. She steadied herself on the slippery rocks, easing slowly towards the grassy verge. Reaching the bamboos, she stood up, breathing deeply, gathering each lungful like a draught of aerial energy. At night the air here was perfect, cool and crisp, as if electrically enlivened by some curious intersection of topography and purpose. She swung around and headed back towards the cave.

She sat in her special spot and closed her eyes, humming softly. When she was ready she opened them again. She looked down at the three pots of colour and picked up the white. Taking a handful of the powdered clay, she crouched low, drawing a long elliptical arc on the soft silt of the cave floor, joining the two ends together with a skilful flourish. The fine white ring enclosed the fire and her large stack of firewood. It curved around her recording equipment and her food supply, encompassing her bower of bright objects - an impenetrable shield, protecting her from intruders. Only those whom she called could enter its magic circle.

The fire had died down again. She picked up a small twig and scraped some ashes from beneath the embers. That should be enough, she thought. Placing more wood on the fire, she knelt down and scooped up a handful of the still-warm ash. Carefully sorting out any lumps of charcoal, she sifted the greyish powder through her fingers, pouring it into the coco-shell containing the now liquefied unguent. She mixed them together with a little water, so many times to the left, so many times to the right, until she had a bubbling lather.

Taking a handful, she rubbed the soapy mixture into her wet hair, massaging it well into her scalp. It was just right. She applied the rest of the shampoo and rubbed it in. The harsh alkalis tingled on her skin like nettles; the oily suds frothing like some mind-enhancing mousse. She looked in her mirror. Her long wet hair curled from the foam like snakes escaping the cranial confines of a gorgon. Dare to look on me, she thought, just dare to gaze into my eyes.

She reached out for the flake of obsidian and placed it in front of her. She looked down at its darkling jet blade. It glinted like some magic dagger, a theurgic kris of black plutonic ice. She picked it up, fingering its sharp glassy edges. She loved the way it fitted her hand, as if made by some dark subterranean twin. It must be done, she thought.

She held the knife at arm's length. Slowly, with a steady rhythm, she began to cut. The serrated blade moved lightly across her hair. Her long tresses fell away as she worked, curling like serpents in her lap. I am only the first, she reflected. In years to come, thousands, millions would follow her pioneering lead, responding to the call within, like ancient seeds germinating to a preordained biological calendar.

Her hair lay all around her. She lathered more of the caustic lye onto her now shortish crop and looked in the mirror. *Coupe sauvage,* she thought with a smile. Taking great care, she drew the volcanic razor across her scalp, shaving in long runs the remaining hair to a low stubble. She ran her fingers over the prickly bristles, irritated by their obstinate presence. It must be smooth, she thought. She took more of the oily shampoo and rubbed it into her skull. She clasped the obsidian blade firmly and shaved away the last of the horrid little glochids. At last, she splashed water over her head and looked in the mirror. It was smooth. Perfectly smooth. It must be kept like this. She stared at the shining orb, feeling a warm flush of satisfaction.

She put down the mirror and knife and gathered the long wavy curls, arranging them into a neat pile.

Picking up the coconut of powdered white clay, she poured a little into a small shell, adding a few drops of oil, stirring it with a twig to a rich glossy paint. She did the same with the red ochre, placing it alongside. The soot she left in its crock, decanting into it the last of the oil to make a thick viscous lampblack. Dipping her fingers in the sooty mixture, she smeared it over her face and scalp, her neck and breasts, rubbing it well into the skin. Adding a little more soot, she massaged the black pigment onto her hips and belly, down her legs to her toes. She looked in the mirror, smiling at her reflection - a melanine madonna, primagravida at term. All was as it should be. She dipped her fingers in the pipe-clay and red ochre. On the dark canvas of her swollen body she drew the patterns of power - waves and spirals, rubrics and uranian spots of white.

When she was finished, she stood up and stretched. She looked around her. The preparations were nearly complete. Now the most important rite would have to be performed. She picked up the coconut shell of white powder and walked, humming softly, her mouth slightly open, to the circumference of the circle. Bending down, she drew the glyphs of invocation on the cave-floor. They will come now, she thought. I am prepared for them.

She lay down again and placed her hair in a thick mat upon her stomach. Using her arms, she shovelled the silver river sand all around her, covering her dark body in a coat of sparkling silica.

She turned to the recorder and rewound the tape to the head. She put on the earphones and flicked the switch. The wind's plaintive song filled her like a lullaby.

She closed her eyes, concentrating attention within. The pulsing sounds floated through her like an elaborate celestial timecode. She drifted towards the place where the future came back to meet her.

THE LABYRINTH

Jamad's heavy-bladed machete thwacked through the underscrub with a crisp efficiency. The long tendrils of spiky rattan fell to the forest floor. Villiers felt a curious pleasure as he stamped on them, twisting them beneath his boots, as if trying to render them harmless. It was a futile gesture. All around them, a dense wall of razor-sharp jungle hemmed them in. Only the constant thwack of their machetes held any reassurance of a safe passage.

Not in his worst nightmares could he have imagined a jungle so inhospitable. In this part of the reserve there were few large trees. Instead, a dense wilderness of malicious palms grew in thick profusion, interspersed with stands of thorny bamboo, or *bambu duri,* as Jamad called it. For hours they had been hacking their way through, the spiny body-arresting hooks hindering their every step. The undergrowth pressed in on them from all sides. Thickets of lantana and pandanus, overgrown with rattan, straggled in every direction. All around them, studded with long needle-like spears, an understory of *salak* grew in close-packed clumps, like the anti-personnel defences of some perverse jungle deity. Scrubby masses of horizontal hibiscus, impossible to push through, spread in front of them, choking their way forward. Drenched in sweat, they fought against the solid barrier of vegetation, cutting a narrow path due north-east, towards the interior.

They had left Mitchell back at the camp that morning. Complaining of stomach cramps, he had lain in his sleeping bag, moaning like a bloated banteng. Villiers was glad to leave him behind. Ever since they had arrived, Mitchell, without being obvious, had done everything possible to counter the ideas that both he and Jamad had suggested. After two days of fruitless searching along the rugged south coast where the unruly breakers of the Indian Ocean crashed against outcrops of broken sandstone, Jamad had suggested they turn west to explore the range of mountains that dominated the skyline. Mitchell had refused. For another wasted day, they had stalked along the thin coastal plain, dotted with stunted scrub and an occasional windblown *gebang* palm, deformed by the constant salt-spray.

"The interior ..." Mitchell had muttered, "…must search the interior ..." Villiers had seen the distinct lack of enthusiasm on Jamad's weather-toughened face.

"*Banyak duri,*" argued the tracker, bemused that anyone would choose of their own volition to explore such a jungle hell.

"It's the one place I never fully explored," insisted Mitchell, "I'm sure she's in there."

It seemed a dark irony that having reluctantly agreed to probe the interior, Jamad and he should now find themselves alone, hacking through its thorny perimeter, while Mitchell lay in bed, groaning like a hypochondriac toad.

Villiers stopped and wiped the perspiration from his face. In the hollow valleys, where the scrub was thickest, the humidity grew unbearable. He looked up at Jamad, slashing into a knotted tangle of traveller-vines and brambles. Jamad's energy seemed tireless. The blade zinged again and again at the tough intertwined creepers. Villiers glanced down at his watch. Midday. They had been at it for five hours. In the oppressive noonday heat the birdsong had ceased. A quiet unnerving stillness hung heavy in the moist air. He picked up his machete and tramped, groggy with fatigue, towards the wiry tracker. At the top of the rise, he stopped again to catch his breath. When he looked around, he saw that Jamad had gone, disappeared through a dark hole in the undergrowth.

Tall shrubby trees resembling wild citrus, with long bayonet-like thorns and dark glossy leaves, grew beside the entrance. On each side, strangler vines and lianas, thick with razor-sharp hooks, curled amongst the rattan in a barbaric display of cruel intent.

The longer he had been in this green hell, the more he had felt a grim apprehension tugging within him. He wasn't yet sure if the source of this unease and growing horror was due entirely to the surrounding hostility of the jungle, or whether it lay closer to home, generated from within his own mind. But whenever it caught his attention, it seemed to coalesce and gather intensity around one particular image. Ensnared as if by a nimbus of rattan and thorns, he saw within him, the dark unshaven face of the man he had come to distrust. It was an image he couldn't shake off, that dogged him like a bad dream. Slowly, as if with premeditated menace, he could see Mitchell raise his camera, and in the curved reflecting glass of the telephoto, he saw the approaching shape of his own death ...

"*Bapak* ..."

His eyes struggled to open.

"*Pak Villiers, Pak Villiers* . . ."

The stillness, the heat, the extraordinary power of the vision, had by some eerie subversion, distorted his sense of identity, and left him with the nagging feeling there was more, much more yet to uncover.

"*Pak Villiers* ..."

As his eyelids opened, he was surprised to discover where he was, sitting amongst the vines at the mouth of the tunnel. He heard Jamad calling from the other side of the thicket, a distant world away. This uncanny sense of falling deep into an inner realm, where time and space dissolved into disassociated images, had increased ever since that day of the eclipse, when by some strange freak of nature, his sight had been so oddly affected.

The high-pitched screech of a shrike shattered the silence. He crawled through the tunnel, grateful for the thick rubber knee-pads he had sewn into his trousers, cursing his lack of foresight in not bringing a pair of protective gloves. With every move, needle-like brambles spiked his hands and scratched his palms to a raw pain. Above him, barbed overhanging hooks snagged at his clothing, tugging him in several directions at once. He heard his shirt rip as he pulled himself free, only to find himself caught once again - the vicious rattan bringing him to an immediate halt.

He reached up behind him, trying to un-snag the serrated tentacles that held him in such a tight uninvited embrace. At once, the rattan hooked his sleeve, trapping his arm at an impossible angle above his head. As he looked up, he saw that his watch had stopped, jammed at a perpetual nonexistent noon.

The sweltering heat thickened around him, drenching his body in a blanket of moist warmth. An insect dropped down his collar and wiggled across his back, crawling along his ribs and ferreting into his sweat-soaked armpit with a sharp thrusting motion.

"*Pak Villiers ...*"

Jamad's voice seemed further away as if he had given up and continued on without him.

Streams of sweat ran down his nose and dripped onto the leaf-litter. A large black ant arrived, quickly followed by another. Within moments, a thin regular column was scurrying back and forth, dipping their mouthparts into the growing pools of mineral perspiration. He watched with a puzzling sense of detachment as they crawled up his one free wrist, swarming over his body in a giddying confusion of legs and antennae. With comparative relief, he felt them nipping at his skin - their fastidious jaws a mild sedative after the sharp immobilising pain of the rattan - but as they released their strong corrosive fluids, a powerful irritant ate into his wounds and his brain spun between searing agony and a dull inexplicable numbness.

They crawled into his ears, nibbling on his lobes, tapping, ever so gently, on the stretched membrane of his eardrum. They crawled in his eyes. They trooped up his nostrils and inside his clothes. They crawled everywhere.

In a distant somewhat muddled way, he noticed he was rearranging his thoughts to accommodate the undignified finality of this unpleasant turn of events.

They would strip him bare, reduce him, trussed in a barbed net, to a skeleton on the forest floor, and then march on. A few decaying bones would mark the spot. There was no natural justice after all, no law higher than the law of the jungle. The universe would propagate generations of army ants and little Mitchells - all busy in their small insectivorous way, to further their own genes. But he refused to give in. He refused to be a victim. Paralysed with pain, even bound and captive, he would fight on. Death would never hold him. In his own way, he would fight on. He would offer his body as food to the ants, a gift to sustain their life force. Turning his attention deep within, he would concentrate, in the intervals between each breath, on the vital essence beyond.

Through the waves of intensely itching, refined, almost insensate pain, he felt he was encased in a cocoon, surrounded by attendants lifting him on high while his internal organs metamorphosed towards their final form. This was it; they would devour him, portion by portion, chomping him with a barbaric reverential hunger. In his last conscious act he would give his body to them. His flesh would become their flesh. It would be a pleasingly unorthodox apotheosis. He would nourish their collective intelligence in return for nothing at all. Offering them the palpable substance of his body, he would slip invisibly through the encircling mesh in a defiant demonstration of faith.

As he stared through the thin film of sweat obscuring his vision, he saw approaching towards him, down the thorny reaches of the tunnel, that face, that same familiar darkly bristling face, and felt his skin creep with terror. In different guises and whenever he was at his most vulnerable, this image kept returning. He shook his head again and again, but still the shadowy imago crept closer, floating towards him like a disembodied spirit in search of a home. The beads of sweat ran down his brow and trickled down the bridge of his nose. As he gazed at the face before him, he saw in rapid succession, the menacing features of the cameraman, half-hidden behind a pair of binoculars, transform into a grotesque warrior ant, cleaning its ever-moving mouthparts with fanatical precision, then dissolve, by some bizarre organic decomposition, into the expression of stern wrath his father had worn on those numerous occasions when he'd transgressed some unwritten family code. He was coming to get him, closer and closer. Between his teeth he clenched a knife. He was almost upon him. He raised the knife like some deranged pirate and swung it down; the blade a silver-grey blur slashing towards him. Their eyes met, and for one brief moment, he recognised a pure unadulterated terror before opening his mouth to scream...

The strident screech of a bird, sliced through the silence, amplifying the moment in his mind.

His breath ... his breath ... He grasped at his next breath and saw Jamad's face pressed close to his, slashing at the rattan with his machete - the tracker's watchful gaze eyeing him carefully as he hacked at the dense spiralling vines.

* * *

Standing in the clearing, he stood naked and shook the last of the ants from his shirt. Jamad crouched low on his haunches, puffing on a *kretek*, his smile occasionally breaking into a full throaty chuckle.

He pulled on his clothes and sat down, taking a long swig from the water bottle. The best part of the day was gone. They had covered very little ground. They had fought their way through the seemingly impassable zones of scrub-jungle and had at last broken free into an area of larger trees with a relatively clear understory. It had been a pointless exercise. He knew that when he saw Mitchell again he would find it hard to control the rage smouldering within him.

A low restless layer of sound hung in the air, more eerie than usual. As he looked out at the surrounding forest, he realised in a confused kind of way, that all day he'd had the unconscious sensation they were being followed. Even now, after hours of crashing through the most impenetrable of jungles, it was impossible to let go of this powerful intuition that they were being shadowed. He tried to shake off the imagination, absurdly paranoid, that somewhere out there in the underbrush, a set of eyes was watching them. Several times he thought he'd heard, above the metallic buzz of insects, the distinctive shutter-click of an automatic camera.

He took another drink and passed the flask to Jamad.

"*Kembali* ?" he asked Jamad, suggesting they return.

"*Ja, mari kita.*"

They stood up and looked around them. It was difficult to tell whether the clearing looked entirely different or whether just some part of it had lost the marginal familiarity it had gathered in the short time they'd been sitting there.

What disturbed him, however, was that Jamad, for once, seemed utterly lost. They crashed around, looking for the opening they'd cut through the undergrowth. An unmistakable edge of desperation quickened the tracker's pace. His smile vanished, all traces of the chuckling prankster subsumed under a deadly seriousness. For what seemed like ages, they stormed through the forest looking for the tell-tale signs of their track, but when they found only the dangling branch of a marker they'd made not long before, they knew they were walking around in circles.

Villiers reached into his pocket and pulled out his compass. He looked at the slowly rotating needle with blank incomprehension, unable for some moments, to discern the precise nature of the problem. The needle continued to spin, seemingly at random, sometimes faster, sometimes slower. His stomach tightened. He knew of particular places on the earth's surface where the normal processes of geomagnetism broke down, where wildly fluctuating fields caused havoc to any attempt at survey or navigation. Jamad peered over his shoulder. They looked at each other. The low chirrup of insects and birds gave no clue to the direction they sought. What little wind there was had died down and they had long ago left behind the sound of the sea. They had stumbled into some strange dark place, some *terra incognita,* unexplored and uncharted, from which return now seemed increasingly unlikely.

Jamad pointed with his machete to a large clump of close-set *salak,* and marched off towards it. Villiers followed. Almost immediately, a vicious tendril of rattan slashed like a whip across his face, its sharp hooks slicing over his cheek and catching with cruel precision his upper eyelid.

"Jamad !"

A loud clicking registered somewhere in the back of his brain.

He reached up and grabbed the rattan, gingerly extracting the hook from the bleeding fold of skin. He could feel that it had sliced into his eye.

Testing, he opened them. A red mist swam before him. It was Mitchell who stood in front of him, the long lens of his camera dangling around his neck.

"Better get you back to the hut, old boy, you're in bad shape."

"The track ... ?"

"Over here, old boy. This way."

THE HUT OF DREAMS

This was the hut he had lain in for so many nights, delirious with fever, unhinged between her sudden passing and the uncertainty of his part in it. A sense of loss, of time spent and gone forever, of opportunity and all prospect shattered, ate within him like a vulture.

Taunted by grotesque misbegotten shapes, he had floated in some semi-conscious blur, unsure of purpose, trying to connect with any surviving remnant of meaning. Night after night he had glided in and out of sleep, drenched in sweat - the horrific after-images of his dreams reanimating before him, charged with a renewed preternatural energy, feeding like rabid deformities upon his mind. He had lain there paralysed, unable to defend himself - his arms and legs heavy and leaden, unresponsive to the commands his brain struggled to send. Hallucinations tugged at his hair, merging surreptitiously with his thoughts. Hideous apparitions grinned and slobbered all over him. A loathsome array of monstrosities paraded before him, autonomous and jeering, tormenting his inability to think straight, poking with unerring accuracy the vulnerable recesses of his being. Their echoing taunts twisted and spun within his head - a dizzying tornado goading him inwards - daring him to uncover the hidden axes around which he turned.

Whenever he closed his eyes, icy fingers caressed him, burning trails of terror across his skin. Fear of confronting, face to face, the ardent dispenser of this glacial touch, petrified him. He couldn't open his eyes. A foul rotting stench filled his nostrils. His eyes clamped tighter. The putrid suffocating breath wrapped around him, stirring, like a charmed kiss, a fetid half-formed image of corrupt resurrection. He lay back, the cadaverous owner of this hag-toothed halitosis fondling his secret desires.

Ages passed. A long terrifying stillness rang in his ears. His body, stretched like some giant fallen tree hacked from its roots, slowly decomposed into the floorboards. The malevolent disconcerting quietness alternated with fits of uncontrollable trembling. Again and again, a sharp involuntary shivering swept through his limbs as he tossed on the hard wooden floor, until, racked by hunger and fatigue, he sank beneath its sponge-like surface, into another, altogether more disturbing world.

Vague spectral images drifted across his field of vision as he tried to remember. A dark screen of anxiety obscured his memory, undermining his ability to recollect. In a way this hut represented the last outpost of his feelings towards her. It was here that he had plunged into that endless interior sea, the black nightmare realm from which he thought he would never return. This was the hut of dreams. It was troubling to be back again.

He looked over at Villiers asleep on his mat, a large medical gauze covering his eye. Shrouded beneath his mosquito net, he looked like some dormant pupating cyclops, mysteriously suspended from the ceiling. Jamad lay snoring in the other corner.

He stood up and walked over to the door. A fresh wind blew in across the ocean, sweeping away the malarial images of the past. He stepped outside and walked down towards the beach. The soft gurgling of the stream drew him to it. Here, the water tumbled down the valley from the mountain highlands, meeting the beach in a series of large meandering pools. He crouched low, watching the mudskippers fling themselves across the shallow lagoon-like surface. He knew he was putting off sleeping in the hut, avoiding, for as long as possible, falling once again under its malignant predatory sway.

He stood up, looking at the half-moon above. He was tired. His head ached. It had been a long day, He found himself walking along the beach, his feet sinking deep into the wet sand.

It was an empty desolate coastline. A strange plateau of weather-shaped sandstone separated the shore from the scrub. Bizarre rock formations, eroded by the sea and wind, carved dark silhouettes into his mind. A continual play of shadows, washed grey-green in the pale lunar light, shifted across the vaguely suggestive outlines. On the edge of the plateau, a solitary *gebang* palm, fans rustling in the breeze, stood resolute against the unremitting elemental onslaught.

To his right, the surf crashed against the sand, the foam swirling around his feet. He walked further up the beach, climbing the rocks to the top of the sandstone bluff. Away in the distance, across the scrubby plain, the shrill high-pitched shriek of a night bird punctured the roar of the sea.

He sat down on a rock and looked out at the ocean. A line of breakers stretched along the entire coast. Above the headland, the moon's white spinnaker sailed towards the horizon. Just visible through the salt-spray, he could see the lamp still burning in the hut - a faint diffuse glow against the dark shape of the highland range. He couldn't put it off any longer, he would have to return. Already he was nearly asleep. He stood up and started walking, weaving through the clumps of pandanus and lantana that dotted the narrow plain. Without warning, a startled muntjac leapt from the bushes, and was gone again, its white hindquarters flashing momentarily before it disappeared.

The flame spluttered low in the lamp as he stood on the threshold looking in. Villiers still lay there beneath his net, suspended in an inexplicable state of levitation. Curled in his blanket, Jamad dozed on the other side.

He sat down on the step and took off his boots. Out to sea, the navigation beacons of a passing tanker caught his eye, distant pinpoints of light through the veils of spray. He watched as they sank slowly beneath the horizon.

Of its own volition, his neck sprang back, suddenly jerking him awake. It was impossible to tell how long he'd been asleep. The lantern was out. The wind blew moist across his face.

He grabbed his boots and went inside.

He climbed into his cotton sleeping bag and adjusted the folds of the mosquito net. The hut's loose thatch rustled as it shifted in the wind. He closed his eyes, feeling his energy drain away. He had spent all morning trying to exorcise the misshapen creatures that lurked within these walls. His stomach had churned with anxiety, tying itself in knots. In the end, he had given up. It had seemed easier to follow Villiers and Jamad through the rattan than rid the hut of its memories. Even now, every little noise and creak seemed to magnify within his mind, conjuring up associations he thought he'd forgotten.

He floated in some half-sleeping limbo, drifting, awake yet not awake, where undeveloped thoughts and sensory perceptions merged, projecting strange vivid fragments of an old semi-processed film.

An owl called from the bush. She was near. He could feel it. He could definitely feel it. The wind rustled around the roof. Away in the distance, the owl called again. She was coming. Dressed like some Queen of Death, she was coming. The wind blew stronger, buffeting the thin walls of the hut. He knew that to see her again was to die, but it didn't seem to matter. There was something he wanted to tell her. The owl called again, closer this time. It was her, screeching through the trees, wings outstretched, talons flexed. She would swoop down on the hut, appearing around the doorway in a flurry of feathers, golden like a winged Egyptian eye, and he would die, consumed in a blinding white light.

He lay in the dark, waiting. A long time seemed to pass. The owl had grown silent. Perhaps she wasn't coming after all. The wind howled around the hut. A scraping sound nearby caught his attention. He sensed her presence. Yes, she was here already. He could feel it. He struggled to open his eyes. His facial muscles somehow refused to obey. A soft delicate pressure touched upon his eyelids. At last, he opened his eyes and saw her.

She sat there in front of him, smiling; her eyes glowing like embers. There was something he wanted to tell her but he couldn't remember what it was. As if she could read his mind, she placed a finger in front of her mouth, quietly hushing him with a gesture of silence. She looked different somehow, but in what way he couldn't be sure. He was surprised how long her tongue had grown, tapering to a thin elongated point like an ant-eater's. She saw the astonishment in his eyes and smiled, drawing her arms around him. He knew it was impossible yet somehow, as they kissed, she whispered something in his ear. He was still trying to work out how, when he realised he'd missed what it was she'd said. Her long pangolin tongue travelled up behind his palate, exploring, all the time exploring, as if licking away the last remnants of volition, devouring each preceding morsel of dream, finally curling down his nostrils and wriggling free, snaking around his cheek towards his ear. She whispered again. It seemed she was talking in another language, some strange jumbled collection of sounds which held no recognisable meaning. Her tongue flicked deep inside his ear. He opened his eyes and she returned his look, her pupils beaming like fire. He could hear her, yet this time he knew she hadn't spoken. At last he understood. I am waiting, she said, her mouth not moving, her eyes dark and compelling. Come to me, I am waiting.

As if a long way away, he could hear the first almost imperceptible sounds of the dawn chorus.

Another voice, somewhere else, spoke quietly, gently warning him. It's a trap, it seemed to say, it's a trap. He made a note not to forget but already it seemed so long ago, and he just couldn't, for the life of him, follow the strands of memory back far enough, back to what it was he had told himself to remember ...

A BROODING SILENCE

Family. The word sent a shudder down her spine. She had tried over and over to reconcile herself to the harm she had experienced from her parents. At best, she found herself wondering what bitter twist of fate, what mean-spirited and wilful oversight had brought them together, such divergent, chronically incompatible personalities. But that was on a good day, when she could get a little perspective on it; for the most part she simmered in a blind seething rage, furious at the thought of her childhood so utterly defiled.

Daddy. Even now the word left a bitter taste in her mouth. She had gone on trusting him, gone on trusting him because he was daddy. And who else was there to trust? There was no one else. No one. She had gone on trusting him because ... because he was daddy and she was his little girl. She was his little girl and he was daddy and she trusted him and she trusted him because ... she trusted him because ... because she loved him.

She looked out of the cave and down the valley. It was still raining. Thin windblown veils drifted into the treetops below. A bank of dark grey clouds was gathering above the western horizon, towering into the dull overcast sky.

She had loved him. And now she hated him. Hate. She hated him. Plain and simple. He had taken her trust and destroyed it. It wasn't fair. It just wasn't fair. And she was only little. He had broken the rules. God, how she hated him.

A skein of wildfowl veed through the drizzle. She watched as they flew up the valley and disappeared over the ridge, heading inland.

Today was the day. Already she had lost count of the number of times she had tallied up the days, just to make sure. She was ready, as ready as she would ever be. This was the day.

It was odd the way just the thought of motherhood made her angry. And yet it did, there was no denying it. It seemed as if mother and anger were part of the same experience, inseparable, indivisible. All those years her mother had turned a blind eye, never saying a word. She was part of it. They were sick people. They were sick people and they would have to pay the price. That was the way it was. This was the day she had chosen. They would never bother her again. She would show them. They were sick people. They would have to pay the price.

Animals knew better. She remembered the duck she had seen, so many years ago; the duck that had first made her want to work with wildlife; splashing about, hanging its wing loosely to one side as if it were broken, distracting attention while her convoy of ducklings scampered to safety further down the river-bank. Protection. Nourishment. That was how it should be. She was ready. Her head was shaved and she was ready, as ready as she would ever be.

Certainly more ready than her parents had been. They had been totally unprepared. Even so, it was no excuse. And her father - with his cine camera and his stupid home movies, prancing about, pretending they were happy. Happy families. Those images, they were all lies. There were no memories to feel safe in, no times to go back to. Only that horrid insistent voice and the intrusive lens of the camera. She would never forgive that cameraman. She found it hard to even remember his name. She turned it over in her mind then spat it out. Mitchell. Yes, that was it, Mitchell. No better than the rest of them. The lowest of the low. He had sided with her father. He would pay dearly. The thought of it brought a smile to her lips.

The clouds were massing overhead, darkening the sky. A low grumble of thunder rolled across the ocean. Electrical storm, she thought, it could disturb the baby. She rubbed her palms over the tight drum of her tummy, soothing away the tension. It was amazing what she had learnt already from the child. They were in constant communication. This was no ordinary baby. This child was special. She allowed herself to feel a warm glow of pride. She had been chosen. Of all people, she was the one. It made sense in a way. All the things she'd had to suffer, all the hurt and pain, all the sadness. Everything she'd been through had brought her to this point of understanding. And yet she knew there were others far more deserving. She was only the first. Here, in this cave, miles from anywhere, a new epoch was beginning. It was a great honour.

The panther padded up to her and curled in a furry ball at her feet. They would be safe here, away from all those prying people. She had chosen it this way. The time had come. She was ready.

THE MIRROR

Villlers stared into the shaving mirror, carefully lifting the corner of his bandage. He peeled away the tape and pulled the gauze from his eye, inspecting the damage. It was worse than he had thought. He could open it only a little, but he could see, between his bruised and swollen lids, the red network of burst capillaries and the dull amorphous shape that had once been the pupil of his right eye. The double scratch marks, already slightly septic, stretched from his cheekbone up into his hair, like rusty tram lines on an abandoned siding. The entire right-hand side of his face and his forehead had turned a dark yellow and had puffed up in the night. Gingerly, he touched his cheek and brow, running his fingers lightly over the swelling.

Sore. It was extremely sore. He looked again at his reflection in the mirror, at the bloodshot shape squinting back at him. He had a dreadful headache.

"Coffee," said Mitchell, passing him the mug.

"Thanks."

He took the drink and put it down on the verandah floor, opening the first-aid kit and taking out a roll of cotton wool.

"Looks bad," said Mitchell, sitting down beside him.

"Yeah, feels bad."

Mitchell raised his mug and took a sip of coffee.

"We should get you to hospital."

"There's no point."

"You could lose your sight."

"Yes."

"Villiers ?"

"I think I already have."

"What ?"

"I think I've lost it already, or at least half of it. I can't see out of it at all."

"Let's take a look," said Mitchell.

He turned towards the cameraman.

"Can you open it any more ?"

"That's as far as it'll go."

He inspected the face just inches from his. It was the closest he could remember being to Mitchell. He studied the deep-set eyes and the faint upturned sneer at the corner of Mitchell's mouth. Deep lines creased his forehead and the sallow skin of his cheeks. Dark shadows hung like a mask beneath his eyes.

"Hmm," murmured Mitchell, looking thoughtful. "So you can't see anything at all with this one ?"

"Not a thing ... a fuzzy greyness, that's it."

"I think you should go to hospital."

"Mitchell, I'm blind in one eye - you want it medically confirmed ?"

"The nearest one's about seventy miles. We could go to the guard base and call for a boat."

He sighed. It was hard enough not to feel that in some circumstances violence wasn't such a bad idea after all.

"It'll heal soon enough."

"Or ... we could walk up the coast. There's a village at the edge of the reserve ... I'm sure they'd give us a ride out."

"I'm not going."

"The boat would be quickest."

"I think I'll just ... stay here."

"You should at least let a doctor take a look at it."

"Mitchell, I'm staying. Okay ?" He stood up and fetched the water from the fire, pouring it into a basin, then, taking a bottle from the medical kit, he sprinkled a little antiseptic into the scalding water, watching the white clouds swirl below the surface. He dipped a wad of cotton wool into the basin, letting it cool for a few moments before applying it cautiously to his eye.

"I'm only thinking of you, old boy."

"Yeah, I know. Thanks."

"I mean it could get infected."

"Let's drop it, shall we ? I'll take my chances."

"Okay, okay. Whatever you say."

Villiers took the cotton pad away from his face and looked at the congealed gunk lodged in its moist fibres.

"Drink your coffee, old man, before it gets cold."

"Right. Thanks."

He looked at the large mug of coffee on the verandah beside him - curdled spots of milk powder slowly circling around its rim. He took a sip. One thing about Mitchell, he could make a good cup of coffee, even though he never did seem able to dissolve the milk properly.

Already he could feel his headache easing.

He took another length of cotton wool and repeated the process, cleaning away the remaining dirt from the wound and wiping the surrounding area.

He reached into the first-aid kit and took out a bottle of antiseptic lotion, rubbing it on the parallel scratch marks that surrounded his eye.

He peered in the mirror. The purple stains of Condy's gave his face a strange camouflaged look, like a wild beast.

He pulled out a tube of ointment and opened it, dabbing white spots along the torn eyelid.

"That should do it," he said, looking at his bizarre reflection. He took another mouthful of the strong sweet coffee.

"You'll need to get some rest - let it heal as best it can," said Mitchell.

"No more than a day. I want to get moving again."

"Where to ?"

He nodded in the direction of the mountains.

"That's where we'll find her."

"I'm not so sure that's wise."

"Why not ?"

"I think we should wait until your eye's healed a bit. Just in case."

"We'll see."

"It might be better to stay in the lowlands, maybe explore the headwaters of the river."

"Maybe."

"We never really looked there thoroughly ..."

"Seen the scissors ?" he asked, rummaging around in the first-aid kit. He took out a roll of adhesive tape and another gauze bandage.

"I've got them," said Mitchell, taking them out of his day-kit and passing them over. "Here you go."

He took them and cut two lengths of tape, placing the patch carefully over his eye, taping it down firmly.

He looked out over the beach to the sea. It was a grey day, drizzling, slightly cold.

He drank the last of his coffee and turned to Mitchell. "So what are you doing today ?"

"Ah, not too sure really," replied Mitchell, "marking time in a way, 'til you're fit. I suppose Jamad and I might take a little mosey in the bush."

"Your stomach pains 've gone then ?"

"Just about."

"I think I'll go lie down."

"Right you are, old man, you get some rest."

"I will."

He got up and walked over to the door of the hut.

"Oh, Mitchell ..." he said, turning to the cameraman.

"Mmm ?"

"If you're going into the bush ... do take care, won't you ?"

"Right. I will. Thanks ..."

Villiers turned and went inside the hut. He sat down on his mat and pulled out his journal. He thought for a while then started writing.

THE STORM

Mitchell followed Jamad around the rocky coastline - the steep jungle-clad cliffs to the right, the furious sea to their left. The south-west winds were blowing hard, straight into shore, whipping the waves to a vicious choppy froth. Mitchell wiped the moisture from his face as he looked out to sea. The wild surf smashed against the outcrops, sending showers of salt-spray high into the air. He was drenched. Not long after they had left, the drizzle had turned to a light rain, gradually falling heavier, and now - mingled with the spray, it was beating down in torrents, soaking them to the skin.

He leapt from rock to rock, trying to keep up with Jamad. It didn't seem to matter how fast he walked, he was never able to match his pace. God, how the little man annoyed him, always pestering him about the price of his equipment, silently toting it all up, expecting some sort of handout. On his first trip here, Jamad had made it known he'd like to have the ring he wore. In a rash moment, just to get him off his back, he'd said he could have it, promising to give it to him the day he left the reserve. As that day had approached, he'd resolved that whatever happened, Jamad would not get the ring. Now, whenever there was a moment to spare, Jamad made some comment about it, reminding him with a sly smile, of his broken promise.

Mitchell looked up at the trees clinging to the cliff. The wind roared in across the breakers, howling around their stunted branches and wizened roots with a wild rustling moan. The underside of their leaves flashed like so many flags, desperately signalling submission.

They came to a gap in the cliff where the fractured wall of rock dropped sheer to the sea below - the waves crashing against it in a thundering sheet of foam. As each successive breaker smashed against the rockface, an enormous green swell of backwash recoiled with a hissing roar, rolling out to sea where it collided with the next incoming wave. Below them, a narrow fissure in the rock formed a natural channel, sending the water rumbling underground to spume from a blowhole on the far side, thirty feet above their heads. It was impassable.

They turned back and climbed the most accessible part of the cliff where a small waterfall wept in a mournful arc to the pebbles below. Using hanging roots they hoisted themselves up, struggling over the ledge at the top - all slippery with moss and algae - to the murmuring stream beyond. Knee-deep in water, they followed the stream-bed for two hundred yards then scrambled up the steep side of the spur, hauling themselves up on young saplings, their boots sliding crazily in the mud. Gradually climbing higher, they worked their way towards the shoulder of the ridge, pushing aside the cold wet leaves as they went.

At last they looked out at the ocean - angry and steel-grey. From his vantage point sitting atop a rock, Mitchell could see, despite the poor visibility, a vast expanse of coast. Exposed to the full force of the gale, he looked out on the wild panoramic view, a turmoil of sea and air, as all around them the trees blustered and bent in the wind, grit and leaves flying in every direction. He scanned around from the south point, where, just on the other side of the hill, Villiers lay recuperating, to the rugged outlines of rock to the west and the dark headlands beyond. He found himself imagining Dominique, walking along this coast, her hair billowing in the wind. Villiers was right. This was her kind of place. Yet he had searched for her here not long after she had disappeared, exploring the range and these western beaches for over two weeks, twice buzzing along the coastline in the Forestry Department chopper. How would he react if he found her here after all this time ? ... if she suddenly emerged from the jungle and walked along the beach ? The thought displeased him, as if by staying alive for so many months, she would have won some personal dispute, some private battle in a strange undeclared war that he had forgotten - perhaps never known - the precise nature of. As he turned it over in his mind, it was something of a shock to realise that he had no longer thought of her as living, that unbeknown to him, a part of his brain had by some strange reverse denial, already exiled her to a tragic death, and that in that unconscious wish he felt the most secure.

She was the anxiety he felt whenever he entered the forest. She was the tightening that gnawed in the pit of his stomach. She was the unpleasant confrontation that lurked half-hidden in the undergrowth. And yet she was alive. He had seen her in his dream. Come to me, she had said, come to me.

She was here, somewhere on this coast.

He turned to Jamad and pointed at the animal track that led around the spur and down the side of the slope towards the shore. If they followed it they would rejoin the beach well past the blowhole, and at the same time, avoid several of the more treacherous looking stretches where the surf burst violently against the rocks.

They made their way down the track, the sharp branches of the stunted brushwood scratching against their shins. Sliding down a loose scree slope, they dropped to the beach - gravel and rocks falling all around them.

The wind hadn't eased; if anything it was blowing stronger, gusting across the waves in cold briny sheets. They walked around the rocks to the craggy needle at the point of the headland where white-water surged across the shallows - a seething carpet sloshing through the rockpools, foaming and bubbling at their feet. On the leeward side of the promontory, they found only limited shelter from the storm, as the sou'wester not only swirled around the point, cold and raging, but curved over the knoll, dumping itself with even greater force on the beach below.

All along the foreshore, a weird collection of ocean-borne rubbish had been blown up on the sand, littering the beach with a tacky exhibition of consumer disposables. After weeks of being in the jungle, the sight of so many reminders of the outside world filled him with disgust. Plastic bottles and lumps of polystyrene lay stranded amongst the driftwood and kelp. Hideously coloured buoys from Japanese fishing boats bobbed listlessly in the receding water, moored by a tangle of net and trawling-warp to a gigantic half-submerged tree stump. An incongruous kitchen mop, its head daubed solid with glossy red paint, protruded from the seaweed, a relic of some distant maritime overhaul. Amongst the debris, the battered bodies of starfish and sea-cucumbers writhed in the sand. One of the starfish, mottled wine-red and white, lay marooned on its back; five arms grimly clutching the large sprouting seed of a *nipa* palm, as if trying to extract the life force from its germinating core. They walked on. Seagulls wheeled overhead. Beached by the storm, a Portuguese man-o'-war sprawled lifeless amongst the litter, its long venomous tentacles, all knotted with transparent globules of jelly, wrapped curiously around an empty aluminium can, as if it had died from some fatal overdose of soft drink.

He followed the tide-line, picking his way amongst the flotsam, while to his right, Jamad searched along the narrow margin where the jungle met the sand.

He checked his watch. Already it was past midday. They would only be able to go a little further if they were to get back to the hut before nightfall. It was an odd dilemma. On the one hand, he felt spurred on by the opportunity to find some clue without Villiers' infernal presence, to best him without his knowledge, yet on the other, he knew that any indication he found here of Dominique's survival would require some radical alteration to his plan. He decided to give it another hour; they would probably travel faster on the way back.

No sooner had he arrived at that decision when, looking down, he saw something that stopped him in his tracks. It was a plastic spool of recording tape, identical to the ones that Dominique always used. The same five-inch reel, the same brand. Lodged half-buried in a mound of sea-weed, its loose tape flying triumphantly in the breeze, it looked for all the world like the remains of some eccentric libation she had tossed to the tide, thrown to whatever local goddess held dominion over the sea.

He bent down and picked it up, rolling as best he could, the flailing tape back onto its spool. He read the label. In Dominique's hand was written; Wind FX, and below it was the date. It had been recorded only eleven days before.

She was here, somewhere on this coast.

He looked around to see if Jamad had seen him pick it up. The tracker was further along the beach, fossicking along the edge of the jungle. There was no way the avaricious little bastard could have noticed. He brushed the last of the sand from the reel and tucked it into his bag.

Casually, he strolled over towards Jamad. It was time to head back to the hut.

THE PALM GROVE

Villiers sat up and stretched. His head was still pounding and movement only seemed to make it worse. But he was damned if he was going to sit in this god-forsaken hut all day. He stood up and walked to the door. It was pouring. In several places the rain dripped through the thatch onto the verandah. He hated this kind of weather; dull, cold, wet. He glanced out to sea. It was a murky grey, as if the journey across the great waters of the Indian Ocean had somehow drained it of its colour. To hell with it, he thought, putting on his raincloak and hat, it's better to keep warm walking than stay cooped up in here all day.

This forlorn, rather lonely stretch of coast had become quite familiar over the last few days. Already he was starting to recognise each individual tree and the characteristics of the surrounding terrain. Clumps of giant pandanus grew everywhere; their long leg-like aerial roots and strange forked branches, topped with spiky growth, reminding him of some fanciful alien invasion. Occasionally he would come across one in fruit - the enormous orange seed-segments dangling in the wind. Others, from last season, had fallen to the sand, their powerful new shoots bursting from the scattered seeds.

He wandered somewhat aimlessly over the dunes, testing his eyesight as he went. Looking continually through just one eye was already starting to make him feel dizzy and several times he had to move quickly to avoid losing his balance.

He turned inland to avoid the full force of the wind, walking over the sand-hills until he came to the scrubby coastal pasture. The stunted brushwood offered little protection from the driving rain and he found himself meandering in and out of the forest margin, from time to time stopping to shelter under a palm. On one such occasion, a kanchil, a type of mouse deer, trotted nonchalantly along the track, oblivious of his presence, and began browsing on some windfall fruit. Very slowly, very quietly, he crouched down, camouflaged behind the foliage. Even from this height, he towered over the kanchil. No bigger than a hare, it moved from fruit to fruit, feeding hungrily. It was such a tiny creature, like an animal in miniature, that the entire rainforest seemed to have shrunk, reduced as he gazed to a world of wonder. The thin white stripes on its neck and front-quarters broke up the fawn outline, glancing across its body like the shafts of light through the forest canopy. Its large glassy eye caught his attention; soft, doe-like, fragile. Then suddenly it was gone, dashing off through the undergrowth.

To his left, a thicket of climbing rattans rustled and swayed, their hooked cirri waving mockingly in the wind. For the first time he found himself allowing what had happened, the full impact of yesterday's events, to sprout into consciousness, growing under closer scrutiny like a field of time-lapse mushrooms.

He had lost an eye. He had nearly lost his life. Were it not for Jamad he probably would have. And Mitchell ... Mitchell had been there. He was now convinced that Mitchell had been photographing him while he'd struggled helpless, enmeshed in the thorn thicket, and again later, at the precise moment when the tendril had slashed his eye. He was sure he wasn't imagining it. The more he thought about it the more certain he became. Like some voyeur calmly watching a death, detached, aloof, Mitchell had snapped him as he'd lain there, no more involved than as if he'd been observing one animal devour another. It seemed the cameraman's obsessions had now reached a nadir, a new depth of scopophilic perversion, untainted by any hint of conscience, a moral and spiritual bankruptcy so complete that mere depravity seemed a positive virtue, beyond which lay only evil, absolute and irredeemable. Yet the overriding thought that dwelt in his mind was not Mitchell's dark motives, not even the loss of his eye, but the persistent realisation that he was lucky to be alive, and accompanying that, as if in tandem, how precious life itself was. That thought alone, it seemed, was capable of miracles.

All around him the palms glowed in a new light, luxuriant and resurgent, dripping with vitality. He felt he was discovering a strange new land, some inner world which time forgot, lush and fertile, enriched by age, exploring its tropical landscape like an eccentric pioneer fumbling his way forward. Half-blind, he would stumble on. He realised that it was he who was now the true photographer, but one who was in the process of turning his lenses inward, testing his latest optical contraption, an experimental telescope, recently invented, whose images, like a mirror on the soul, could capture the intersections of time and fate.

He walked further along the trail, emerging from the dark understory out onto an area of pasture, a kind of grove, in which a colony of giant *gebang* palms had established themselves, their enormous fan-shaped fronds whispering in the wind. He had forgotten about this grove, discovered a few days earlier, and it occurred to him that some unconscious wish to return here had been at work, guiding his feet, drawing him back to explore more fully its wide open spaces. On each tree, the majestic crown of fronds dropped all the way to the ground, a full ninety feet below, its lower half clothed in a skirt-like thatch of dry rustling leaves. The wind eased a little. He looked around at the *gebangs*, growing like a herd of immense vegetal hedgehogs, frozen in mid-migration. This bizarre monocarpic species dominated the grove to the exclusion of all others, an entire field of younger palms surrounding the gigantic trees at the centre. He strode out into the pasture, picking his way between the massive frond-covered trunks, surveying, as best he could, the scene all around. For a moment, the sun burst through the clouds, drenching the glade in a vibrant golden light. He found it difficult, with his restricted monocular vision, to maintain a perspective on things; the palms seemed to surround him in a continuous three-hundred-and-sixty-degree tableau. He could feel their energy all around him, vibrant, glowing; each individual palm a sentient being, alert, upright, colossal in size, a living totem of a supreme power.

As he walked further into the glade, the palms grew larger, encircling the central grove like a gathering of winged tribesmen, listening intently to their respected elders. For a time he felt attuned to this strange silent sermon. On every side, the palms swayed in the wind, creaking and scraping, their fans rattling like antennae, grateful recipients of some invisible agency, whose rhythms he was now beginning to sense. He wandered on. These awesome trees, their large leathery fans sprouting from the soil like the tail of some botanical phoenix, had awakened in him a sense of mystery, an appreciation of the ongoing cycle of life and death.

He walked out into the centre of the grove where three gigantic *gebangs*, taller than all the rest, towered overhead, each at a different stage of inflorescence. In the first, the flowering bract was only just starting to push beyond the crown; while on the tree to the other side, the massive terminal panicle, over ten feet tall, covered in millions of tiny cream-white flowers, had burst from the growing apex in a spectacular display - like an enormous floral tribute. Hanging down the trunk, the fronds were already starting to wither, as all the plant's accumulated energy rose up the stem, concentrated solely into the act of flowering.

In the middle, the third palm had already flowered. Devoid of all leaves, its bare column-like trunk, patterned with an ascending spiral, was topped with a huge bract of ripe fruit. Occasionally, whenever the wind blew stronger, the olive-green drupes fell in a sporadic rain to the earth below. Nearby, several older palms had crashed to the ground, expended, their grey trunks soft and rotting, teeming with insects.

The wind had picked up again, driving dense sheets of rain into the grove. The enormous fruiting branches above him waved in the breeze, as if they too could, at any moment, topple to the ground. He suddenly noticed how cold he felt and wiping the rain from his face, turned and walked back towards the hut.

THE DELUGE

"H*ujan, hujan, hujan,*" said Jamad, as he looked out from under the canvas flap of their tent at the sheets of torrential rain. He turned to Villiers with a smile and gave one of his characteristic chortling laughs. Villiers watched as Jamad took out a *kretek* and lit it with a flourish, exhaling a thick cloud of aromatic smoke out into the downpour. In the four days since they had returned to the river, to search its upper reaches, Villiers had grown fond of the impish tracker with his broad smile of loose teeth and a penchant for practical jokes. Only this morning, Jamad had placed a half-drowned bush tick on the edge of a plate of rice, and with a conspiratorial wink in Villiers' direction, passed it over to Mitchell. In a rare show of good humour,

Mitchell had risen to the occasion, poking it carefully with the handle of his fork.

"Yes, could be *Amblyomma crenatum*," he'd said, "a species of ectoparasite found only on the rhino, quite rare in fact."

"*Ja, sangat manis,*" replied Jamad, doubled up with laughter. Very sweet.

Villiers couldn't help smiling.

"*Dari mana, Jamad ?*" Mitchell inquired.

Jamad waved his hand behind them, pointing emphatically up the hill. "*Seribu meters.*"

Mitchell had looked thoughtful as he placed the tick in a matchbox and resumed his breakfast. He wolfed down the last of the rice and stood up. "Think I'll go for a stroll," he announced, putting on his rain-cloak. Jamad was still giggling as Mitchell pushed past them into the pouring rain. "See you later," mumbled Mitchell.

"*Ja, satu tidak cukup,*" laughed Jamad, as Mitchell had disappeared through the downpour towards the hill.

Jamad sat puffing on his *kretek*, its spiced aroma filling the tent. "*Musim hujan mulai,*" he pronounced sagely.

Villiers stared at the water dripping from the ridgepole of the tent-fly. It had been four days of nonstop rain. The ground around them had turned to mud and the river had burst its banks. The southwest monsoon had well and truly begun.

In the last twenty-four hours, Villiers had become convinced that Mitchell had led them here, to this sodden catch-water, miles from anywhere, for some twisted reason of his own. Clearly Dominique was not here. They had inspected every hillock and rivulet and any other likely place they could find, but all they had discovered was an odd assortment of pig nests, crocodile lairs and rhino wallows. He had begun to suspect that Mitchell was intent on some sardonic test of will, or some perverse delaying tactic to see how far he could divert attention away from their aim.

Villiers looked down at his scratched hands. Even now it felt as if ants were crawling all over his skin. He leant against his pack and stared out at the green wall of dripping vegetation. He rubbed his eye. It was still sore. The eye-patch made it hard to gauge distances, giving the view a flattened, disorientating lack of depth.

Jamad began to hum one of his Sundanese tunes, low and monotonous.

The continuous pattering of rain against canvas was beginning to have an almost hypnotic effect, slowly soothing away the frustration of enforced inactivity.

In front of the tent, a steady trickle of water dropped onto the leaves of a large jungle fig. The constant rhythmic splosh seeped into his mind, saturating his entire psyche with a sense of powerful determination. He would soon be with her. Nothing would stand in his way.

He had made up his mind. As soon as Mitchell returned from this little tick-finding foray, he would demand they paddle back to the watch-tower, to resupply and reconsider their plan.

Jamad lit another *kretek* and flicked the match out into a puddle.

Above the din of the rain he could hear the squelching of Mitchell's boots returning through the mud. The sound grew closer then tramped around the side of the tent. Suddenly Mitchell thrust his face through the tent flap and looked at them with a mad gleam in his eye.

"You'd better come 'n see this," he said, "looks like we got trouble."

"*Apa ini* ?" asked Jamad, getting up.

"*Badak*," replied Mitchell, "*badak mati*."

They put on their cloaks and hats and followed Mitchell out into the rain. They sloshed through the mud and clomped their way up the slope, the wet foliage splashing cold against their skin. Mitchell pushed through the soaking fronds into a small clearing at the top of the hill. There in the mud, a large rhino lay sprawled in a grotesque position, drops of rain splattering against its lifeless opaque eye.

Villiers looked on in horror at the appalling sight. The rain drummed mercilessly against the rhino's mud-spattered hide. Its animating force withdrawn, the heavy grey hulk had collapsed into a contorted heap, legs splayed apart, its neck thrown to one side. It was the head he found most difficult to look at. A deep red wound where the horn should have been was dug into the rhino's nose.

The other two were already inspecting the corpse at close quarters. Jamad showed Mitchell the bullet hole on the rhino's flank.

"Half a mile from camp ..." said Mitchell in disgust, looking up as Villiers approached. "They must have landed on the south coast to avoid detection, then come directly inland. With the wind blowing that way ... and this rain ... no wonder we didn't hear it ..."

"Locals ?"

"Who knows ..."

Jamad was studying the footprints around the body.

"*Empat orang laki-laki,*" he said,

"Four of them," said Mitchell.

Villiers looked at the others.

"I think we should head back," he said.

Mitchell stared at him, unanswering, a cold look in his eye.

Villiers turned to Jamad. "*Mari kita kembali.*"

Jamad shook his head. "*Saya pergi sendiri,*" he replied, "*Pak Villiers terlalu pelahan-lahan.*"

"Too slow ? *Tetapi di prahu ...*" argued Villiers,

"*Pak Villiers ... silikan ... saya pergi terus ...*"

"Listen," said Mitchell, "Jamad needs to get the other guards, it'll be quicker if he goes alone."

"And us ? We're chasing poachers now ?"

"We could lend a hand."

"Forget it, Mitchell."

"Listen; let's just wait 'til Jamad gets back ... see what happens."

Villiers heard himself groan at the thought of yet more delay.

Jamad was already disappearing through the wall of vegetation. They set off after him, following his brisk trot down the hill back towards the camp. They didn't catch up with him until they were back at the tent.

"*Kembali soré,*" Jamad said, slinging on his rucksack and waving good-bye.

They watched him vanish into the undergrowth.

"It'll be evening at the earliest," muttered Mitchell, "more likely tomorrow morning."

Villiers looked over at Mitchell; a grain of rice had lodged in his stubble and hung there like a grazing maggot.

The prospect of being alone with Mitchell, even for a day, seemed suddenly more unpleasant than any chance meeting with poachers.

THE SWAMP

The rain had begun to ease. Mitchell looked over at Villiers, crouching in the corner of the tent, writing his goddamn journal. "Fancy another search ?" he asked.

"She's not here, Mitchell," Villiers replied.

"You don't know that."

"She's in the mountains. I keep telling you, she's in the mountains."

Mitchell stood up. "Then I'll search on my own."

"Where ?" asked Villiers.

"Downriver. The rain'll 've turned a lot of those lowlands to swamp."

"So ?"

Mitchell looked at him carefully, "This might sound a bit morbid, but ... something… may rise to the surface." He watched Villiers take a deep breath. "You coming ?"

Villiers put down his pen. "Yes," he replied.

* * *

Mitchell steadied the *prahu* as Villiers got in. He shoved the boat out into the current and pulled himself onboard.

They paddled downstream. The river was cluttered with broken branches and clumps of vegetation. Several times they had to get out of the *prahu* and manoeuvre its heavy wooden hull over the fallen debris. It was slow and tiring and he could see the wisdom of Jamad's overland return.

Paddling quietly, they surprised a large herd of wild pig grubbing along the riverbank. They edged alongside the nearest myopic boar - its long tusks and spade-like snout furrowing the waterlogged soil like a plough. Engrossed in its forage for fern roots, the boar remained unaware of their presence.

They glided past and the boar looked up in shock. Giving the alarm with a loud grunt, it scampered off into the underbrush. Most of the company vanished into the forest, but one of them, wallowing in the shallows, plunged into the river with a high pitched squeal and swam towards the other shore.

"Damn good swimmers, pigs," said Villiers.

"Yeah," Mitchell nodded.

Bloody idiot, thought Mitchell, what do you know about animals ?

The pig scrambled up the far bank and snorted off into the jungle.

The *prahu* slid downriver. In some ways, the oppressive fears he had felt about returning to the dark interior of the reserve had now dissipated. He could allow himself to relax a little. His overriding sense of anxiety had vanished. He would do what he had to do.

They came to a low-lying area where marsh and jungle merged into a dense tangle. The river had poured over its banks, flooding the surrounding forest in a broad sheet of water the colour of ink. Mitchell steered the boat through a thick curtain of creepers into the dark cathedral space beyond. Clumps of vegetation swirled in the current. Palm-heads sprouted from the surface, their fans waving madly in the breeze as if trying to lever themselves from their submerged trunks and climb to higher ground. The floodwaters stretched out around him. Pushing through the overhanging branches, Mitchell felt a compelling certainty about what he must do. There was no turning back. He had reached his conclusion only after hours of careful self-scrutiny. He watched as Villiers paddled clumsily in the bow. They glided like a ghost ship over the dark glassy surface. The unmistakable call of a coucal echoed in the canopy above.

Avoiding the submerged logs, Mitchell steered the boat through the undergrowth out into an open space - clumped with sedge and marsh-reeds. Here the forest run-off and river had converged, inundating the existing wetlands and creating further vast tracts of swamp.

The dull grey sky seemed bright after the dismal glades of the flooded forest. The rain had stopped.

Spread before them like a luxuriant vegetal carpet, the bright green pads and white flowers of water hyacinths floated on the torpid surface of the marsh. They paddled the *prahu* through it, the bow-wave slicing the buoyant mat like a blade. Mitchell looked behind him at the torpedo-shaped pods bobbing in their wake. A startled jacana, its bronze wings flashing, waddled off in the opposite direction, hopping crazily across the floating leaves.

A wall of reeds and swamp-fern rose out of the water before them. Pushing through this wilderness of ferns and bulrush, they headed over to the far shore where a breeding colony of herons perched along the skeletal branches of a dead *Eugenia* tree.

One after another, the herons rose into the air. Squawking noisily, the birds hovered and swooped above the tree, waiting for the intrusion to pass. Villiers pointed at some fallen timber where the swamp joined the jungle and they paddled around the nesting site towards it.

Here, a section of the bank had subsided and several large trees had crashed into the marsh, separating one swamp from another.

"Try and get through ?" inquired Villiers.

"May as well," he replied.

Mitchell turned the *prahu* alongside one of the fallen trees and clambered out onto its trunk. He steadied the small craft for Villiers as he too climbed out. They hauled the boat out of the water, guiding it through the labyrinth of branches.

The fall was so sudden, it was as if he felt the cold splash of the swamp-water before he realised he'd slipped. He surfaced and saw the startled concern on Villiers' face transform into a look of horror. He felt an annoying rubbing sensation against his leg.

"Mitchell !" screamed Villiers. "Watch out !"

A vice-like weight hung to his left boot, twisting his ankle and dragging him underwater. He knew instantly what it was. He thrashed wildly at the surface as he felt himself being pulled below. So this was it, he thought, death by crocodile; no fears, just a few mild regrets and slow silent suffocation. A strand of pond-weed, suspended in the rays of green refracted light, hung mockingly above him. He was surprised at the complete absence of pain in his leg; only the growing burning sensation in his lungs hinted at the finality of his departure.

Then suddenly he was on the surface again, gasping for breath. In the periphery of his vision he saw Villiers diving into the swamp. He flailed around and felt the solid presence of a branch beneath his grip. In a wild flurry of spray, he saw Villiers whacking the crocodile's snout with a length of wood.

He climbed up through the thick tangle of branches and looked down. Below him, Villiers swam towards the tree-trunk and lifted up his hand. He saw the long thin wake closing fast, the serrated scales on its back clearly visible.

"Mitchell !" cried Villiers, waving frantically, as if determined to shake his hand. It was an odd sight. He looked down at the outstretched palm - beckoning, begging for assistance. Clasped firmly behind his back, he felt his own fingers tighten just a fraction.

"Mitchell ! Help me !"

The croc's jaws opened in a supremely elegant display of dental ingenuity.

The look in Villiers' eye was not to be missed.

He watched as Villiers' tortured grimace slipped slowly beneath the dark reflecting surface. The rippling white shape of his eye-patch finally disappeared.

A koel called from the edge of the jungle; its harsh almost mechanical refrain echoing across the swamp.

The last of the bubbles trailed off into the distance.

"So long, chump," he said. "It's called survival of the fittest."

He climbed over to the boat and lowered it into the water. Picking up the paddles, he eased himself down into its reassuring hull. He turned it around and paddled back towards the tent.

THE TORNADO

The time had come. It had come and gone. She looked down at the ptisan of nettles brewing on the fire, rapidly approaching the boil. Steam rose in long elegant strands from the surface of the simmering green liquid. It was overdue. The baby was overdue. It was the one thing she hadn't anticipated. She breathed in the aromatic herbal vapours. For a day now she had taken nothing else. She poured some of the pungent infusion into a coconut shell and waited for it to cool. Patience, she thought, I must be patient.

The ache in her back was troubling her again. Whenever she sat still for any length of time, her entire lumbar region seemed to ossify and seize up. In the mornings, or after one of her naps, it was an agony just to move. This morning it had been particularly bad. Only after reaching around and rubbing the small of her back as best she could, had she been able even to get up. With a supreme effort of will, she at last managed to roll over and had crouched there, immobile, on all fours, waiting for the pain to recede. It had been some time before she could crawl over to the fireplace, scrape away the ash and once again breathe life into last night's embers.

Ah, nettle tea. There was nothing quite like it. The first sip was always the best. The clear sharp taste tingled over her tongue and raced like fire to her stomach, spreading warm sustaining waves of well-being throughout her body. She had come to love the delicate flavour, its curious blend of gravel and tangy freshness. She couldn't imagine what she would do without nettles. They had provided nourishment when there was nothing else. The bushes she used stood over eight feet tall; a single plant keeping her in tea for days. When she had first discovered them, (it seemed so long ago), one unprotected touch had virtually paralysed her, raising enormous welts on her forearms, blistering the skin to her elbows. It had taken nearly a week to fully recover. Now, wearing two pairs of socks on her hands and using a long sharp pole, she had no trouble gathering the silvery leaves and bushy side-shoots.

She took another sip, staring into the fire. Over the months, she had noticed a distinct greenish tint begin to colour her skin. This strange chlorosis had frightened her at first. She wasn't sure if it was due to her high intake of nettles or whether there was some other problem, something more serious; anaemia, malnutrition, a complication. She had imagined the worst. Perhaps something was not quite right. For days she had dwelt on it. And then she understood. Or rather, she didn't understand but it no longer mattered. She had seen it. She had seen it and it was special. In her vision she had seen it. From that moment she ate all the nettles she could. They were rich in essential minerals; silica and calcium. It was important to give the child a head start. The pigmentation would help. Transplanted to her own tissues, the green cells would help. She didn't know how but she knew they would assist the process. That was the main thing. To assist the process.

She stood up, stretched and walked over to the entrance of the cave. At this time of day, as late afternoon turned to evening, the sun shone directly into the cave-mouth. Every day without fail, it was her habit to sit on the large slab of rock that lay like a fallen obelisk at the entrance - half-hidden beneath jungle creepers -

and bask in the sun's rays. She climbed up the side of the rock, hauling herself up by the natural handholds in its surface. It was almost impossible to do this now but she insisted upon making the effort. It was always worth it. Strangely, now that the baby's head had dropped into its final position, relieving the painful restriction on her diaphragm, the climb felt easier than it had last week. She reached for the rope-like vine that dangled over the edge and pulled herself up onto the slab. Several skinks scampered out of sight, their bright blue tails flashing. Carefully, she stood up and walked, crablike, her hands as extra feet, over to her special spot - a smooth indentation in the grey quartz-seamed surface. She sat down on the warm rock and looked out to the valley below.

A slight mist hung above the treetops, nestling in the leafy furrow that marked the position of the stream. She breathed in. The rain-washed air smelt of mud and vegetation, with a slight trace of salt. Gliding on the warm breeze, a sea-eagle swooped low over the canopy, its white under-feathers turning gold against the sun. It poised in mid-flight then circled round in a wide spiral, its wings occasionally beating, before heading off along the palm-fringed coast. All to myself, she thought, the whole coastline, the entire jungle, all to myself.

She watched as the panther padded up the path below her, leaving deep pugmarks in the fresh mud. They trailed behind, newly-written, like a mysterious overlapping language; encoded, indecipherable, known only to her. Since that morning when she had first woken up beside the panther, there hadn't been a single day when the two of them hadn't sat together, silent, watchful, looking out to sea. She owed this cat everything. It had nursed her back to life when she herself had given up. And it had fostered her will to live. There was an understanding between them, a curious reverse imprinting, yet she knew that by taking the place of the lost cubs she had also fulfilled a deep need of the panther's. The cat looked up, alert, eyes meeting hers. It blinked, then bounded up the rockface and came over to where she sat. Nuzzling up to her, the cat rubbed its nose along hers, its stiff whiskers tickling her cheek. It knows, she thought, it knows. The cat rubbed her again then curled up on the warm slab at her feet, its eyes half-closed to the setting sun.

Out on the horizon, a waterspout was snaking its way towards them. This place, jutting out into the ocean, seemed to attract them. Blown by the prevailing westerlies, they would spin into the outstretched arms of the bay, whipping over the reef and across the lagoon, tearing a trail of uprooted palms through the forest before blowing themselves out further up the valley. She loved watching them. Once she had seen three of them, one after another, roar across the water and rip through the jungle, tossing broken branches and debris high into the air. One had reached the waterfall and for a brief moment, as the cliff-face was swept dry, the twisting tower of water had exploded in a perfect circular rainbow, a halo of prismatic light.

She looked down at the dozing cat. From this angle, in this light, the spots on its fur were clearly visible, black rosettes on a dark chocolate brown. Its paws and whiskers twitched involuntarily as it slipped away, dreaming its catty dreams. She smiled. He was coming. She knew it. The cameraman was coming. He would have to hurry. There wasn't much time. He would have to hurry or it would be too late.

Already she could hear the hissing roar of the twister as it raced across the waves. She looked up just as it reached the reef, vacuuming cascades of foam from the rocks in a strange inversion of gravity. It gathered speed as it tore across the shallow lagoon, parting the waters as it went, drinking the rock pools dry, sucking vast clumps of seaweed, crabs, fish, all, into its hungry funnel. She watched as a long white fountain of spray shot from the top of the spout and fell back to the surface in a graceful parabolic curtain. The tornado, as if renewed, charged up the beach, flinging sand and driftwood in its wake. It ripped into the forest, thrashing the treetops into a loud rustling frenzy, scattering a shower of branches and dead palm-fronds high above the canopy. And then suddenly it was gone, spent, a fine rain of saltwater drifting back to earth.

THE WESTERN RANGE

Mitchell pulled in the paddle and clambered out, mooring the *prahu* to a branch. He hurried up the track to the tent and threw what he needed into his day-pack. He would have to hurry. He only had a few hours start. Once Jamad and the others returned and found him missing, they'd lose no time in trying to follow him. And they were expert trackers. He would have to outwit them.

He looked at Villiers' pile of belongings. Worth a rummage, he thought, dragging the large khaki pack towards him. He opened the flap and pulled out the jumble of clothes. Ah, his torch; yes, he'd have that; rice, coffee, sugar; his knife, definitely his knife; an extra packet of matches, they would come in handy; and aha, a secret stash of mint cake ... so, holding out on me, were you ? you mean bastard. Christ, and what have we here ? a flask of bloody brandy. He whipped the lid off and sniffed it. Brandy alright. He took a quick swig. It was Armagnac. He knocked back another mouthful then stuffed the flask into his pocket. Thank you, old boy, there'll be a little celebration tonight. Pity you won't be able to make it. He felt around in the bottom of the pack and pulled out Villiers' journal. This'll be interesting, he thought, pushing it into the side pocket of his knapsack; bedtime reading.

He put the clothing carefully back into Villiers' pack, folding it neatly and took another look around the tent. Nothing untoward here. Those stupid guards, they'll probably think the poachers have got us. He smiled at the thought. Opening the tent flap, he stepped outside, slinging his knapsack over his shoulder.

He unsheathed his machete and cut the large basal folds from two fallen palm fronds, then punched a series of holes in their fibrous skin with his army knife. He threaded a spare pair of bootlaces through the holes and wrapped the leathery leaf sheaths around his boots, tying the laces as tight as he could. This'll get me over the first bit, he said to himself, tottering clumsily up the track to test them out. They left tracks, but so unusual and so camouflaged as not to be obvious. He adjusted the shoulder straps of his knapsack and set off.

He followed the trail around the bottom of the hill, taking care wherever he could, to avoid the mud, stepping only on the larger leaves and fallen branches that littered the forest floor, looking behind him all the time, checking that the tracks were well disguised. When he reached the stream, just to make sure, he staggered along the stream-bed for a further hundred yards, the boat-like galoshes slipping crazily on the algae-covered rocks. When he felt he'd gone far enough he steadied himself on top of a water chute, sat down and took them off. He stripped out the laces, put them in his pocket and tucked the clog-like leaf sheaths under his arm, wading up the stream for another few minutes before tossing them as far as he could into the surrounding jungle.

He followed the stream up the side of the hill, splashing through the shallows, jumping from stone to stone, dog-paddling across the deeper pools, not once stepping from the watercourse. From time to time he would have to clamber up a waterfall, hauling himself, dripping wet, over the cold cascade at the top, making sure any tell-tale marks in the mud were well covered.

They would never track him. As far as the guards were concerned, he would have disappeared. For all the world he would cease to exist. He would do what Dominique had done. Vanish. It would be easy enough, when the time came, to slip down the south coast unseen, travelling overland, through the mangrove swamps of the isthmus, back to civilization.

The gradient was getting steeper. He was leaving the foothills behind. Suddenly, a wave of exhaustion hit him. Every step became an effort. His knees no longer seemed able to support his weight, yet he kept going. He had to find a place to sleep.

It was getting dark. The sun, long obscured by the massive range, would be close to setting. He pushed on. Already it was getting difficult to see. The water felt cold; his wet clothes clinging uncomfortably to his skin. It didn't surprise him to discover he was shivering. He rubbed his arms, exploring yet another clearing for a dry patch to bed down in. This would do, he thought, looking at the carpet of damp leaves and palm fronds in front of him; not perfect, but at this time of day, good enough. He slung off his knapsack and pulled out his groundsheet, laying it over the leaves to make a rough mattress. Taking out his towel and change of clothes - all carefully wrapped in plastic bags - he quickly changed.

He lit the lamp and climbed into his sleeping bag. A job well done, he thought as he lay down, stretching out his limbs. He was surprised how natural killing felt; the complete lack of remorse or any sense of guilt was a refreshing reversal of his expectations. And, of course, he hadn't actually killed anyone; circumstances had merely prevailed; the crocodile had been hungry; Villiers had been in the wrong place at the wrong time. The more he thought about it, the more elated he became. The perfect murder, he thought; no witness, no weapon. Not even a corpse.

He had often imagined, whilst filming, that he held a certain sway over animals. Many times, he found he could anticipate their movements, and, by adopting various mental strategies and diversions, that he could manipulate them to obey his commands, steering them into a more photogenic position. Dominique too, had a sixth sense when it came to knowing how an animal would react and her ability to communicate commands was if anything, even more highly developed. Villiers' unfortunate demise filled him with a particularly warm sense of satisfaction. It was as if nature herself had somehow read his mind. Responding to his unstated wish, the croc had risen to the surface at precisely the right time. The teeth marks on his leg seemed a small price to pay.

The moon, near full, rose above the forest. He rummaged around inside his bag and pulled out the mint cake and Armangac.

"Here's to you, old boy," he heard himself say as the pale green-blue light rolled across the lowlands. He took a swig, grimacing as the alcohol hit the back of his throat. He rolled over and ferreted around until he found Villiers' journal. He pulled it out and opened it at the first page.

CIRCLES AROUND THE MOON

She felt herself twitch and woke with a start, the rock cold beneath her back. She could hardly move. Her entire torso from her hips to her shoulders seemed paralysed and numb. Even the warmth of the cat, snuggled up alongside, had done nothing to alleviate her sense of total rigidity. If only she could swing her legs to one side she would be able to prop herself up, but to even try sent great swords of pain shooting down her thighs. It was as if her hips had completely calcified and set. An urgent feeling of blind panic swept through her, gripping her in the possibility that she may be stuck on the rock until the very end, lapping at rainwater until she wasted away - a long slow descent into starvation. She looked down at the cat. It was fast asleep. What if she couldn't get up ? And the cat couldn't bring any food ? What would happen to the child ? She looked out into the night, gripped by this new horror. Her heart raced. She could feel a thin film of perspiration on her brow, cold in the chill night air. What was it Villiers constantly kept telling her ? ... breathe ... breathe deeply ... let it go ... She always resented him saying this - as if her cares, her worries were somehow too insignificant, too unimportant to be dwelt upon in any depth. She preferred to explore them fully, not just let them drop in midstream, unresolved, like an echo bouncing down the walls of a well.

She inhaled reluctantly. A sense of equilibrium settled slowly within her. She began to feel solid again. As she lay there, gazing out to sea, an impression of monumental immobility washed through her, serene, implacable. She felt like a great basilisk, hewn from living rock, watching the stars dip beneath the horizon. It was obvious. The resourcefulness, the determination - all the effort which had kept her alive so far - weren't meant to be wasted. She had struggled for too long, fighting doubt and hunger, every kind of discomfort and pain, just to give up now. And after all, she had an obligation. She must see it through. She had been graced with a task. There could be no question about it. She would fulfil her duties.

She breathed out ...

Her fears seemed to subside, to dissipate into the night.

In a few moments she would stand up, as simple as that, and climb back down to the cave.

The sky behind the dark outline of the range glowed with a pale brilliance, as if just on the other side of the hills, some quirk of nature had allowed a small portion of daylight to continue on into the night.

A breeze rustled through the vegetation surrounding the rock. The wind had stiffened a little. The branches creaked disturbingly. She felt cold. She gave her arms a brisk rub. Any minute now she would get up.

She took another breath. Breathing. It was difficult remembering to concentrate on something so simple.

The moon rose above the ridge.

Immediately, the cat looked up, as if some instinctive second sight had perceived the exact moment the moon's light had fallen across the rock. Its eyes reflected a pale icy blue. It looked away then began licking itself vigourously beneath the chin; its head bobbing up and down with an energetic rhythmic motion as if there was nothing more important in the world than grooming that particular patch of fur. It turned then rubbed its forehead against the ball of her foot. She loved it when it did this. Nothing could feel more wonderful, more luxurious; a foot massage like no other. She wiggled her toes into the panther's soft coat. Ahh ... it was ecstasy.

She lent back on her elbows and watched the moon sail free from the silhouetted trees. Not quite full, she thought. The day after tomorrow. That's when it'll be. The day after tomorrow.

The cat kept butting its head against her foot, curling its ear under her toes each time it rubbed. It was strange how just moving her toes seemed to have restored the sense of feeling to her limbs. In a few moments she would get up and go back down to the cave.

She threw her head back, watching the moon float across the sky. Two large rings, like rainbows but paler, softer, glowed around its shining orb, refracted in the moist upper atmosphere. Muted colours played on their edges, aureoles of delicate, almost extra-sensory hues. Already the moon seemed smaller in the sky. It was good to just lie here, letting her mind drift, thinking of nothing at all. She breathed in again, feeling the air slowly fill her lungs. It never failed to amaze her, the difference it made to apply even a little awareness to her breathing. Her head seemed so much clearer, lighter, more free. Feeling the twin currents of air flow in and out of her body seemed to connect her to the outside world, to bring it inside her, while at the same time, remove her from it, distance her in a way that somehow fortified her, made her feel strong, almost invincible. But time and time again, her thoughts would undermine that feeling, burrowing insidiously like worms into the fabric of her being.

She remembered the satisfaction she had felt hurling the film cans at him, seeing one strike him in the teeth, knowing it had hurt. It wasn't enough. Even the pleasure she had derived from exposing some of the rushes, stomping them underfoot, didn't seem enough. What did a man ... no, she couldn't call him a man; he wasn't a man - what did someone like that deserve ? There was no doubt about it. He would pay.

A naked fury howled through the dark spaces in her mind.

A long time seemed to pass. The sound of the sea, far below, washed through her, carrying her out beyond the feelings of hatred she had for him. There were other things that were more important. What happened to him was beyond her control. Creation, or whatever moved through it, had a habit of taking care of people like him, of seeing they got whatever they deserved, whatever was necessary. Yet she knew that her thoughts, even her unconscious thoughts, could tip the balance. It was this that troubled her. To have to bear the responsibility of every dark secret thought that passed through her mind seemed somehow to be asking too much. All the destruction, the havoc ... can one ever really tame its source ? All the darkness that poured out of her so continuously, unchecked and unfiltered ... could it ever be pulled back in, converted into something more useful ? It seemed her mind was like some wild animal, infinitely more dangerous than anything that lived here in the jungle, some dark creature that could never be tamed, that could never be trusted or believed, but only held firmly on a powerful leash and taught the most basic of lessons. The more she thought about it the more convinced she became she could afford no participation in Mitchell's fate. It was his. He would have to face it alone. Yet even now she couldn't be sure whether what she'd seen that day on the island, so long ago, when the python's hungry smile had been slashed, torn by an utterly more terrifying vision, was in fact a premonition or the seed to events that she herself had sown. And he was coming; she had summoned him. There was no going back on that. It was part of the arrangement. She was inextricably entangled. There was simply no getting away from it. He was on his way.

She felt tired. It was a burden to be able to see the future so clearly, to see the whole range of possibilities and to have to modify and adjust accordingly one's actions and behaviour, trying to circumvent the worst of the possible scenarios that the images depicted. But she could now see there was no avoiding what she knew to be inevitable.

At times like this she felt like Nemesis herself, all powerful, weighing the souls of each memory as they floated in front of her before finally despatching her verdict; only this time, it was her own soul she was judging, and try as she might, there was no escaping her evident guilt.

She could hear the coconut palms down on the shoreline, their leaves sighing in the wind. A train of long diaphanous clouds, luminous in the moonlight, blew in across the bay while further out, on the horizon, a formation of thinner darker streaks, like the prongs of a gigantic sky-borne fork, hurtled towards her, breaking up and multiplying in the freshening breeze like a squadron of angry hornets.

She stood up.

There was so much still to be done, so many last-minute arrangements that had to be seen to. All the hundred and one things she still hadn't found the time for. Little things. Important things. Everything seemed so unfinalised, incomplete. All the preparations she had been working on appeared so glaringly inadequate. She was already walking over the rock before she realised it, propelled by the powerful sway of her thoughts and the urgency of the task before her. She bent down, steadying herself before climbing over the edge. The cat padded after her, crouching down on the slab as she lowered herself to the ground.

"C'mon puss, let's go ..."

It jumped down, landing with a quiet thud beside her. So much to do. Rearranging. Finalising. She would be busy all night.

DARK TRANSIT

The disconcerting sensation of being somewhere unfamiliar and not quite knowing where or when, of being unable to put together all the necessary pieces to locate a definite sense of time and place clouded his consciousness for what seemed like an inordinately long time. It appeared that the absence of these vital coordinates, in some way subverted his sense of identity, threatening to rob him of existence until he could finally resolve the dilemma. And yet he found he could think clearly, like a floating disembodied mind. Did it mean then, that there was no absolute being, no pure identity except in relation to a specific place, no sense of self without a known past ? Or was it the opposite ? The experience was similar to those occasions when he had woken in a strange bed, struggling to recognise a familiar item in the room, or when half-asleep, facing an unaccustomed direction, he'd expected a wall to be on the other side from where he'd found it; except this time, it wasn't a room he was in, it was the bush. He knew he was in the bush, he could smell it, the rich, unmistakably earthy smell of rainforest, but of the many jungles he'd spent a night in, he simply had no idea where this one was. Nor had he been asleep, he had been thinking, thinking about something … something that now seemed to have escaped him. The lamp began guttering noisily at his elbow. It all came back. He knew instantly where he was. He realised he had been staring at the same page for longer than he could remember, his eyes swimming in and out of focus, his mind veering off at tangents, wondering what on earth had possessed Villiers to write such a strange journal. He found it difficult to believe that Villiers could have put his thoughts down in the way that he had. They were such an odd couple those two, so curiously different yet alike, so uncomplimentary yet at the same time similar. He had seen, on occasions, an undercurrent, a hint, a vague suggestion of the hidden dynamics of their life together, and it seemed to him that it revolved entirely around frustration, not sexual frustration, although he had no doubt that that too played its part, but in a more complete sense, as if they - and only they - could hinder each other's growth in such a full and thoroughly comprehensive fashion. Page after page he had read of Villiers' journal and still it was the same: the poor deluded bastard, pouring his heart out to someone who he knew would never, in a million years, be able to reciprocate.

He'd probably done them both a service.

But it was Villiers' speculations about the real reason for Dominique's disappearance that had really disconcerted him. If it was true, surely he was the father ?

He let the book drop to the ground and rolled over, blowing out the spluttering wick and settling back down into the comforting nest of his thoughts.

The moon had slipped down over the other side of the ridge. The night, intensely black, wrapped around him. Nothing moved. It was very quiet. Even the stars were hidden by the thick curtain of vegetation above, and what had been shadows when the lamp was on, now merged into a continuous sea of darkness. The sharp edges of his camera dug uncomfortably into the back of his head. He turned over and pushed it further down into his pack. After some time, when his eyes had adjusted, he imagined he could just make out an occasional shape of one of the surrounding trees but the effort became too great. The more he strained to peer through the inky blackness the more convinced he became that his eyes were playing tricks on him.

He sprawled out on the groundsheet, wide awake, thinking about what lay before him. It was an impossible situation. He could now see the inevitability of her disappearing into the forest. With hindsight, the curiously entangled matrix of their lives, the three of them, had made it perhaps the only course of action that she could take. It was clear; the entire series of events had been as meticulously planned as a military strategy, a charade, as carefully thought out and as compulsively enacted as a child's game, a mere excuse to wreck vengeance not only on Villiers but on him as well. The thought of it sickened him. For a brief time, his world had seemed enlarged; the hollow ache in his stomach had been cured. He had tried to grasp onto it, eager to preserve the illusion. But no more. The last traces of that illusion were now going, evaporating into the night. He could feel his mind racing ahead, even now anxious to avoid what he could see was coming. Ever since he had found that tape flapping in the breeze, he had tried to forestall this moment, when his mind would turn to the conscious recognition of what had been fermenting quietly below the surface. For he knew there was only one possible solution. He felt his mind grow calm, as if reaching a clearing in the jungle. There could be no more procrastination. It would have to be done. He would have to complete the job.

THE FORBIDDEN GARDEN

The flames leapt in the small circular fireplace. She often came here at night, lying in the shallow waters of the pool, watching as the firelight danced around the foliage. Orange coloured reflections, laced with red, shimmered on the surface, transforming the pool to a vat of molten metal. She stared at the fire. It was the first thing she'd built when she had originally planned this garden, hollowing out the centre and laying the stones end to end. She had no idea why; it had been an impulse. As she turned it over in her mind, she couldn't stop herself laughing. It suddenly seemed wildly amusing that in an area devoted solely to the cultivation of plant-life, she'd built something so inimical to growth. Her laughter fluttered through the canopy like the wings of some fledgling lifting into flight. She listened to the sound it made in the trees, a brittle lilting tremolo merging into the sustained sibilance of the wind in leaves. Small coppery waves splashed around the edge of the pool. Piled high, the fire burnt with a delicious ferocity, crackling and hissing as the resinous sap boiled in the flames. The water felt cool around her ears. Leaning back, she dipped the base of her scalp beneath the surface and lifted her hand above her head, watching the beads of golden fire stream down her arm. Her entire body seemed aglow. She imagined she was bathing in a tub of liquid gold, her limbs being gilded a little more each time she slipped beneath its surface. Every day the layer of gold grew thicker and every day her body became a little heavier. Now that she had become so large, so heavy, she was convinced that the process was almost complete, and that within her, a solid curiously-shaped nugget of the precious metal was gradually replacing her internal organs, transmuting her flesh and blood into something radiant, something indestructible. Or at times, particularly on nights like this, the water turned to blood, a pool of blood, warm and pungent, to enrich and tonify her skin, and she would lay there, sipping its metallic taste, visualising the donors and their exact manner of giving.

Far away, as if coming from beyond the surrounding wall of trees, a strange cackling sound, like a night bird, jarred in her ears but as soon as she became aware of it, it stopped.

Impulse. Impulse and imagination. They seemed such dubious assets. Still, one must work with what one has, she told herself. There was no point trying to change the way it was. That would be disastrous, fatal. Besides, it had been the right thing to do. The ashes she'd spread around the roots, raking them into the topsoil with her digging stick, seemed to have had a positive effect on the plants, stimulating them into a vigourous new growth. It occurred to her that by feeding on the burnt mineral remains of other plants, her vegetable charges were, in effect, partaking in a rudimentary but nonetheless brutal form of cannibalism, soaking in the nutrients that only shortly before had been living cells. And the life ? she wondered; when all these mineral salts move from one form to another, where exactly does the life go ? It seemed such a great puzzle ...

There were so many gaps in her understanding. She felt a burning need to know more, to be able to put all the pieces together so they at least made sense. There were times when she felt she was working completely in the dark and that to have even a little more knowledge of the great forces moving inside her would have been helpful. But there was no one to ask, no books she could read, and to see it as anything more than a difficulty, to acknowledge it as a problem, would have been to admit to a defeat so crushing as to be unthinkable. Creating this garden had been her way of trying to resolve the situation. She had long since ceased to regard it primarily as a source of food but saw it now rather as a kind of barometer, intricately poised between two worlds, between the forces of nature and those that dwelt within her, an indicator of how she was faring and at the same time, an omen of things to come. Here, in this tiny jungle plot, she could study the biological processes at work and exercise with growing confidence her capacity to nurture.

She'd had such difficulty at first. Gardening had never been her forté. Her few previous attempts had all been failures. Everything she touched seemed to die. Villiers used to laugh about it, saying she had brown fingers. And certainly, on those occasions, it was rather odd the way each plant appeared to take exception to her. In one extreme reaction or another, they had all expressed radical disapproval of her treatment. Some had shrivelled and withered as if blasted by an icy wind, some had simply turned yellow and languished or become rotten, others were plagued by a series of mysterious diseases. There were so many things that could go wrong.

But here, months ago, when she had first started, she was determined to get it right, and with an almost religious fervour she had cultivated the soil, digging in leaf-mould and an enormous quantity of rhino manure - collected by the sackful from the huge hill-like dung heaps that the animals deposited along the forest trails. On each side of the stream, in a clearing dominated by *langkap* and the fish-tailed *sajar* palms, she had constructed a terraced descent down to the central pool, sculpting the earth into an elongated horseshoe like an immense botanical amphitheatre. It was a natural suntrap. The entire area she had mulched with leaves, and to make sure there was enough water, built an intricate system of canals and dams that steered a small but constant flow along the inner wall of each terrace before trickling down to the next level and back to the stream.

The humidity that built up within this area was intense, a damp heat that steamed out of the soil in rich pungent clouds, yet at the same time, balanced by the cool presence of running water and shade. It was a garden within a garden, a greenhouse within the greater greenhouse of the rainforest, a small patch of paradise where she could learn the long-forgotten lore.

But still the plants refused to grow. Nothing she could do could coax them into life. Each seed she had sown had failed to germinate. Each cutting she had struck, every sucker or transplanted sapling had wilted or withered, rapidly turning a disheartening brown.

Only a profusion of toadstools and stinkhorns sprouted from the dark earth, taunting her with their strange shapes.

It was clear a sacrifice was needed.

From the moment she'd had that thought, things had started to improve. The plants began to grow, visibly, with a quickness that had startled her. New shoots had appeared, bursting from the stems one after another until soon the whole area had been transformed into the lush image she'd originally had in mind.

Now, all around her, everything sprouted with tropical vigour, an exotic collection of wild growth.

A betel nut had been the first to germinate, its slender stem rocketing towards the canopy, spraying new fronds from its central apex almost daily. Already it had formed a trunk; smooth, green and unblemished, girdled with a ladder of pronounced white rings. She had experienced such joy when that first tall seed-leaf had appeared and although she knew it had little to do with her, she couldn't help feel a sense of achievement. It seemed so regal, so glorious in its habit, that in her mind it had become inextricably linked with the child. Several times, as she lay in the cave at night, she had had the same reoccurring dream, seeing the palm sprout from her belly, the arching crown of leaves rapidly giving way to small fragrant flowers while at the same time showering her with golden egg-like fruit. She had only to open her mouth and swallow one of them to see it too shoot from her belly, replacing its predecessor in a perpetually regenerating grove. This vision of a new genesis with her at the very centre had now revisited her dreams so often that it seemed all was as it should be, a fitting exaltation of her true role, so that any sacrifice needed was but a small price to pay. In appreciation for such a good omen, she had erected at the foot of the tree, a small shrine of speckled rocks that she kept washed and scrupulously clean, every day adorning it with a fresh selection of jungle flowers.

The cuttings too, had seemed to acknowledge the new arrangement. A papaya tree, tall and elegant, like an elongated umbrella, shot skyward, its slim trunk patterned with a mesh of interlocking eyes where the old leaf-bases had fallen away. She had found it by a stream, knocked over by a rhino. Its lower half chewed to pulp and its leaves lying in tatters. Hauling it up the slope, she had trimmed away the shredded ends and set it upright in the earth. Within no time at all it had sprouted and now stood almost twelve feet high, several suckering branches bursting from its base.

Another of her first successes was a young transplanted banana. Responding to the enriched soil, it was already starting to fruit. A green hand-like clutch of fingers sprouted above the dangling peduncular remains of the flower. To help the fruit develop, she had tied a large plastic bag - found on the shoreline - around the flower-bract, and although it looked incongruous and somewhat ugly there was no doubt it was working. The fruit was ripening.

Around the perimeter of the garden, in a high hedge-like barrier that was intended to keep out muntjac and browsing rusa deer, she grew her nettles.

Nettles, bamboo shoots, hibiscus flowers, *salak*, the thirst quenching rattan fruits, wild lemons, almond-tasting fern shoots, ginger, turmeric root, a kind of swamp cabbage, several species of edible figs, pepper-leaved vines, *nibung* nuts, and a large number of green herbs she didn't know the name of, all flourished in her garden or its immediate environs, providing her with a wide range of tastes to augment the sago and coconut staples.

But it was sweetness she craved above all others.

A large *sajar* palm had one day burst unexpectedly into flower and as the long burgeoning spadix had approached maturity she had lopped it off, collecting the sweet liquid jaggery as it poured from the wound. It produced far more than she could ever hold in her modest supply of containers and often, in the heat of the day, she would lie beneath its feathery fern-like fronds, resting in the shade as the half-fermented sap dribbled slowly into her mouth

From then on, she had learnt to tap other palms; *nipa*, *kawung*, *langkap*, even the coconut, and on long walks through the forest or along the coast, their energy-rich syrup had been a life-saver. There was nothing quite like it.

But it was the soft milky-white jelly of young unripened coconuts that she loved above all, their delicate flesh melting on her tongue.

She lay back in the pool, the sound of water tinkling in her ears. Something moving in an overhanging branch caught her attention and she looked up. Half-obscured amongst the foliage, an indeterminate shape clung to the branch. The leaves moved. A dark masked face stared back at her, the firelight flickering in its raccoon-like eyes. A long tail flicked furiously from side to side. She smiled. It was a familiar sight. This particular palm civet, (she was sure it was the same one), often sneaked into the garden at night, drinking the sweet toddy as it flowed from the cut stumps, dangling from the fronds in a spectacular display of arboreal acrobatics. It looked down at her with an alluring rather wistful expression - then satisfied it was in no danger - set off along the branch towards the dripping palm, its tail curling like a question mark as it grappled for balance amongst the leaves. She was always pleased to share what she had with this engaging, rather smelly nocturnal visitor.

In a way, the garden now represented an enormous problem, a paradox, for its luxuriant foliage, its sheer success, was a constant reminder of the covenant she had agreed to, and a reminder therefore, of her meddling with an equilibrium of forces that she knew to be already perfect. Her interference with this delicate order had become increasingly difficult to justify, yet she knew at the same time, that the promise she had made could not be broken. There seemed no way to extricate herself from this position nor to reverse the particular turn of events.

On the other hand, she couldn't deny she experienced a great thrill holding these lives in such a fine balance. It reminded her of the first time she had slept with another woman, a delicious warm sensation of delving on the other side of a taboo. And whenever she allowed herself, she felt that the distance between her and the deity had now become infinitely reduced, so that at times she was a goddess herself, amaranthine, presiding over destiny like an old hand.

She looked over at the mounds of dark earth that stood on either side of the hole. She had spent all night digging the grave and she was exhausted. Besides, she told herself, there was a difference between interfering and being prepared.

THE LAIR

He opened his eyes. The difference between having them shut and having them open was so extraordinary, so confusing, that for what seemed like a very long time he just lay there, opening and closing, staggered at the beauty of so much light. Again and again it shone like a pinpoint in the distance, then swirled in luminous fast-approaching clouds, enveloping him in a warm mist of well-being. It came in wave after wave of soft colour, glowing and fading and glowing again. He was travelling into it, swimming, gliding, as if down a radiant never-ending tunnel. What was confusing was that it was brightest when his eyes were closed.

The glow seemed to fill his head and wash through him, a quiet unavoidable light, searing with a fierce gentility at the surplus cargo in his mind. He was speeding into it, faster and faster, feeling it dislodge large segments of his life, projecting them with a precise clarity, like a beam from some other dimension, beyond thought, beyond judgement, out into the open, as if on a vast screen where for all to see he was reminded of his relative insignificance, a small speck of transparent dust, imperfect, impure, dwarfed by any comparison.

He stared into the centre of the tunnel, the walls of light rushing by. A sensation of ever-increasing velocity and simultaneous stillness swept through him. He was tumbling, falling, as if drawn irresistibly towards some distant all-attractive source. The possibility occurred to him that he was already dead but it seemed so absurd he found himself laughing out loud. There was no death, there was no darkness, there was only light, a vast sea of light. He became aware of the sound of his own laughter and opened his eyes. Instantly the vision disappeared and again he was lying in the cold wet mud, the walls of the lair glistening with larval glow-worms.

The water rippled around him. It lapped over the soft fetid floor where he lay, splashing with a quiet persistence against the mauled remains of his boot. The bleeding had stopped. He had no idea how long he'd been there but he could sense the growing thinness of the air.

The smell was overpowering. Old bones and a slurry of decomposing flesh oozed beneath him, seeping into the mud with an unbearable stench of decay. A rib stuck uncomfortably into his side. He tried turning around but discovered he was wedged tight, jammed against the roof.

His fingers, trapped beneath his chest, squelched in the mud, clawing for space. He looked over to the mouth of the sump where the roof of the lair sloped down into a narrow passageway before disappearing beneath the water. He tried wriggling towards it, pushing with his foot against the wall. It was no use; he was stuck.

He remembered the look in Mitchell's face. He could still see the faint curl at the corner of his upper lip. It had surprised him that such an extreme emotion as hatred should seem so cold, so indifferent. The pale green water had closed over him. He felt again his feet being dragged down, heavy beneath him.

It irritated him to realise he was wasting his last moments thinking of Mitchell. Yet he felt sorry for him. There was something so pathetic about Mitchell, like a lost child - a little boy gone a little bad, forlorn, without guidance or the benefit of human warmth. It struck him that beneath that strange grim persona Mitchell was someone who was immensely sad, trapped from his future, as if an impossible set of circumstances had hardened around him, freezing him like a snapshot in a distant past event. He could see the desperate necessity behind the lens, behind the constant quest for extreme images, as if by capturing these, the cameraman might unlock some private matching memory, some arrested part of himself and finally set it free. His searching for sequences in the world of nature; for images that followed a pattern, were but substitutes for a lack of meaning. Until some experience, powerful enough to restore a sense of worth, could fill the emptiness inside, Mitchell would never feel complete. It occurred to him that Dominique had been that experience for Mitchell and that her disappearance had affected him in some primitive way he could only guess at.

Dominique. She had always wanted children. When the doctors had told her it was impossible she had cried for days. But there was no longer any doubt in his mind. He knew a miracle had occurred. It no longer mattered to him whether it was he or Mitchell who was the father. What mattered more than anything was that he be there. With her, with the child.

He felt the air stretching thinner in his lungs. He was breathing deeper now, trying to cling to every last molecule. Suffocation. Suffocation. For as long as he had known her, Dominique had held an intense and increasingly morbid fear of being buried alive, and yet at the same time, had a peculiar obsessive fascination for the subject. By some quirky repression, she had been unable to pronounce the word 'asphyxiation'. No matter how often it was repeated out loud, however carefully, she never got further than half-way, incapable of fixing the strange collision of consonants at the beginning of the word to its suffix. There in the middle, as if at a crossroads or private Golgotha, the letter 'x', like an insurmountable barrier to pronunciation, strangled every attempt. It was only much later, after they had been married for over five years, did she tell him. Her father had taken a pillow and tried to smother her. She had been six. He discovered at the same time she could never bring herself to use that number, it held a type of magic, a dread spell, an age she preferred to forget. Six and eleven, they were her numbers. Six and eleven.

At times their lives together, their very similarities, the intensity of their relationship, had been overpoweringly claustrophobic. But he knew after all that had happened, after all they'd been through; he knew now, like he'd never known before, that he loved her and he always would.

He realised that death itself no longer held any fear for him; he had felt it and gone beyond it, transcended it and left it behind. It was the thought of dying without seeing her again that was unbearable; without ever seeing the child, without ever knowing it, without ever playing with it; laughing, guiding, teaching - all those things within him he longed to share.

He looked up at the roof of the burrow. Every grain of silt and clay seemed magnified, bathed in the pastel light of his ecliptic vision. The glow-worms clung to the roof like stars or hung by long sticky threads, as if trawling for his last coherent thoughts.

He was surprised how calm he felt, no panic, no sense of unease.

He took a long deep breath, summoned up his strength and pushed hard against the wall. There was a soft squelching sound from the direction of his feet but no movement. He tried again. He knew that beyond the submerged entrance to the sump lay a passageway - five, ten, perhaps fifteen feet long and beyond that, the swamp. And he estimated it couldn't be more than twenty feet to the surface - probably less. If he could pull himself through the passageway he might make it to the surface.

He tried again. He kept on pushing, harder, harder. He would get out of this hole, he told himself, or he would die trying. The air now was desperately thin and, with the exertion, he was already breathing fast. He checked himself and took another long deep breath, visualising his arteries, his cells filling with the last of the oxygen. His head was slowly exploding. His lungs were burning. His whole body was on fire.

His foot, with a suddenness that surprised him, slid free from the mud. He felt himself sliding down the slope towards the oily ink-black water. He dug his fingers in and managed to stop himself inches from the edge, gazing down at the reflection below. For one moment he was unsure of who it was, seemingly just beneath the surface, and whether the dark face that stared up at him had come to fetch him back or was there to bar his way forward.

The glow-worms swam before his eyes, reminding him, in some obscure way of his mother's death. He had never realised it until now but his love of swimming, of diving, was directly connected to her death. Unconsciously, as if daring the water to take him as well, he was trying to be with her, and all his attempts at breath control were mere exercises in delaying the inevitable. He saw it now as a kind of dangerous undersea roulette, a rigged game in which a part of him expected to lose but was addicted to nonetheless. Plunging into the unknown, defying the odds - it was his way of embracing a death that he knew would reunite them forever.

This was it. He closed his eyes. Instantly the light was there again, glowing softly. He filled his lungs and slipped below the surface, pulling himself along the yielding mud, kicking hard against the walls. The pressure on his ears was deafening. Like some marine mammal about to be born, he scrambled along the passageway. He pulled himself forward one last time, suspended in the final moments of his final breath. There was nothing to lose. He was ready.

THE FEVER

Mitchell wiped the sweat from his forehead and tried to clear his mind for the next stage of his plan. It had taken longer than he'd thought. He should have been there by now. Instead he had wandered through the jungle for two days, hallucinating, lost, attacked on all sides by that horrid green light as if trapped by an army of triffids. Whenever he lay down and looked up at the immense trees with their buttressed trunks crawling with aerial roots and the forks of their branches dotted with epiphytes, he sensed he had stumbled into a kind of overgrown prison complex, a new experiment in penal reform, monstrously landscaped by some demented designer. He would lay there for hours, sinking deeper and deeper into the lush green carpet of moss, convinced of the injustice of his incarceration, trying to determine his bearings from the lengthening shadows. He had heard about these institutions, located on islands or in dense jungle, a tyrant's answer to political activists and dissidents. Too tired to move, he came to the conclusion that by some typical bureaucratic confusion he had been mistakenly consigned to the psychiatric wing, thrown into solitary confinement for subversion when his only crime was love. Those chortling men with their pressed camouflage uniforms and dangerous machetes had somehow tricked him. But he was innocent. He was the last surviving inmate in a long-forgotten work-camp, the victim of an insidious totalitarian response to his lone dissenting voice.

Mitchell tossed another branch onto the fire and huddled a little closer to the spluttering flames. The damp wood burnt slowly, giving little comfort to his shivering limbs. He had woken up yesterday morning with that familiar malarial sweat covering his face and could tell by the way every muscle ached that it was going to be a bad bout. But he had known worse times. This was nothing to those months he had spent crashing through the forest when she had first disappeared. He gazed into the flames, intent on gathering all the available heat from the pale fire.

He was keeping a sharp eye on those lianas and epiphytic ferns. He would keep them under observation for as long as it took. They irked him. They seemed to creep towards him. He had realised at last, that the foliage was sprouting from his mind, but as he looked at the bizarre large-leaved shapes he was unsure how much comfort he could draw from this discovery. Yet he was beginning to favour the heightened states he experienced in this reoccurring sickness. They seemed in some way more real than what usually passed for normality. And they brought with them an unmistakable lucidity; a way of seeing, a kind of pictorial language that could probe the darkest corner, uncovering new connections, constructing a series of windows from a seemingly haphazard assortment of events, creating an improbable synthesis from the unlikeliest material. More than anything, he enjoyed the fluid, rather random access it gave to those parts of his memory that he didn't normally explore.

He could remember it as if it happened yesterday. He was only four. He had wanted an ice-cream. His mother had said they were going home and it would spoil his appetite. He had started screaming in the way that seemed to upset her so much. In the end she relented. She pulled the car over to the kerb and stopped. 'What flavour ?' she had asked. 'Chocolate,' he had replied, deliberately refusing to say please. His mother had looked at him in the severe rather resigned way that she reserved for such lapses in manners. She shut the car-door and locked it carefully behind her. He fiddled with the straps of the seat belt, pushing at the red button. He still hadn't figured out how to get it off but he was working on it. He watched as she walked to the ice-cream shop. He could tell by the impatient way she bustled along the pavement that she was fed up. He took a simple delight in irritating her. 'You take me for granted,' she used to say, 'you treat me like dirt.' He watched as she walked out onto the crossing. A black car, travelling as if in slow motion, threw her across the bonnet and over the roof. He knew instantly, long before the dark puddle spread across the pavement, that she would never get up again. He found it hard to believe that a car travelling so slowly could do so much damage and as he thought about it he noticed he was screaming, not in the way that irritated her, but in a new way, a way he'd never known before. He fiddled with the red button, throwing his full weight against the straps, kicking against the seat, struggling to get free.

He had sat there for hours, alone, watching helpless as people clamoured around. Eventually an ambulance had arrived and taken her away. He remembered that more vividly than anything - her body being lifted on a stretcher into the back of the ambulance; the doors closing and the ambulance driving away, disappearing around the corner. The moment before it vanished was imprinted on his mind, indelible yet a little blurred, like a frame of film frozen in mid-action. The crowd stood there, talking for a while then gradually moved off down the road. Nobody noticed the little boy in the car - parked just fifty yards away.

It all made sense. Perfect sense. He could see now that motherhood was somehow sacred, a state of existence separate from any other. To defile it was to break the unwritten rules and be punished. He accepted it - he was being punished. His whole life had been a succession of punishments for causing her death. He knew that. But he also knew that Dominique was capable of anything. It was up to him. It was he that would have to protect the child. She was dangerous. It was up to him to stop her. She had done it before and she could do it again. That was what Villiers had never understood. Villiers. That self-righteous bastard. He thought he knew it all.

Mitchell stared into the fire. There were things he knew about Dominique that in seven years of marriage Villiers had never found out. The demons. They were real. She had said so herself. The rituals she had described … Although her father had done it many times before, she had been eleven when she had conceived. Two pregnant women in the coven had performed the operation. He remembered how she had cried as she told him what had happened next. How her father had included her in it - had made her do it. They had stood in a circle and passed the portions around, right to left.

She had cried as she told him, but he now knew it was a ploy. She could never be trusted. She was possessed.

He would protect his child. That was his duty.

If there was a price to pay he would pay it. He had loved her - he still loved her - and that was why he must kill her.

THE LIGHTHOUSE

Villiers trotted along the path at a steady pace, ignoring the pain. The mud was already drying to its usual soft dampness. When he had got back to the tents he had found Jamad and the other guards huddled around the radio, listening to the news of a series of massacres in the eastern provinces. All interest in capturing the poachers appeared to have vanished as they sat glued to report after report of the atrocities and the spiralling sequence of events.

Villiers had grabbed what supplies he could from the stores and filled his pack, setting off for the coastal track via the lighthouse to the western beaches beyond. Preoccupied with the news-bulletins, the guards had barely noticed him come and go.

As he ran, a troop of macaques crashed through the branches overhead, scattering to the higher reaches of the canopy. Twice he had to side-step snakes as they slithered across the track. At last he rounded the corner to the watch-tower and scrambled up the wooden stairs.

Lifting the trapdoor and stepping inside was, for a brief moment, a peculiar, somewhat disorientating experience. After weeks in the rainforest, the empty room with its bare floorboards and broken windows seemed an extravagant luxury, yet it exuded a welcome almost homelike quality. But there was little time to savour it. He headed for the small storeroom and filled his pack with all the food and medicines he could carry. The leaf-nosed bat was still there, dangling from the rafters, watching him with its studied indifference.

He ran along the coral path across the mudflats, his boots crunching beneath him. Large crabs scuttled noisily out of the way. He burst out onto the beach and again was taken aback by the familiarity of the scene, as if this bay with its tranquil waters and wading egrets represented some kind of safe-haven after the terrors further inland.

He waded across the estuary and climbed the steep bank to the grazing pasture beyond, where a herd of banteng mooched amongst the scrub. The entire pasture was choked with lantana and it was some time before he could push through to the far side and rejoin the coastal track.

His forehead had been badly scratched in the bushes, adding to the septic geometry that already chequered his face, and as he adjusted his eye-patch and wiped away the blood, a peacock screamed from the treetops, reminding him of his strange dream and the bright metallic bird that had perched upon the drowning whale.

He set off again at a fast trot, trying to pace himself against the hunger and exhaustion that he knew weren't far behind. For days now he had been unable to pick up any signal from her and this worried him. Since he had first arrived in the reserve, he'd relied almost entirely upon these instinctive hunches in his attempt to understand what had happened; and in their absence, an irritating sense of doubt seemed only too ready to replace them. To reassure himself, he tried to picture in his mind the scene he might discover when he found her. He knew this birth, so unexpected, so late in life, would have unleashed such powerful conflicting forces within her, that withdrawal to the wilds was probably the only way she could have felt safe. It would have ensured a privacy; a sense of security away from the threat of people, away from the threat of men and her own unpredictable reaction to them. He guessed that whatever it was that had happened between her and Mitchell had in some way precipitated that dark cloud of guilt that so often hung over her. It was anger that had always been her first line of defence against this guilt and against the introspection and hurt that accompanied it. But he was now convinced that here in Ujung Kulon, with no voices other than her own, she would've gathered the strength to meet that hurt, and in her own way to triumph over it.

Yet this jungle, the entire topography of the area seemed to have an unsettling subversive effect upon those who came into contact with it for any length of time. Already he had found himself fantasizing about the watch-tower and the gentle waters of the surrounding bay, imagining a quiet retreat for himself and his new family. Perhaps they could recuperate there before returning to the humdrum domestic routines of civilization ? Or if they couldn't get the necessary permissions, perhaps they could slip further into the forest ? - united at last; Dominique leading the way, showing him her favourite places of shelter and food.

He shook his head as if to clear these annoying distractions from his brain and increased his stride. The wound on his ankle where the crocodile had pulled him under was now starting to really hurt. His sock was wet and red with blood. His eye was pounding. Already he found himself wondering if he could sustain this pace for much longer. His legs were aching; his stomach was a hard knot. But he couldn't stop. He knew that if he did he would never find the strength to restart. This cross-country marathon to the lighthouse - the extreme westernmost tip of the province - was the last hurdle. If he could get there, perhaps grabbing a quick bowl of rice from the lighthouse keeper on the way, then press on, down to the great coastal stretch beyond, he was sure he could find her.

He ran on, conscious of the steady beat each footfall made on the track. At last he began to pass small clumps of papaya and cultivated bananas that he knew must represent the outer perimeter of the lighthouse garden. Tiring now, one foot in front of the other, he raced on, up the long inclined slope to the bamboo fence, through the gate and up the stairs; banging, banging on the lighthouse door for someone to answer.

THE EYE OF THE DAY

The sun streamed through the cave-mouth, slashing large chunks of orange light from the darkness. She had slept all day. She rolled over, surprised at the intensity of the pain. She waited for it to pass; then stood up, again surprised, this time by how completely it had left her. She stretched and walked to the entrance, watching the sun begin its plunge into the sea. *Matahari,* they called it here - the eye of the day. Soon it would be dark. She started humming to herself, a low rhythmic hum, monotonous, over and over again. Her feet, of their own accord, followed the rhythm, half-stepping, half-pausing, resting between each cadence. Her body swayed, shifting weight from one hip to the other, rediscovering instinctively the steps to an ancient dance. It felt better this way; moving, gently moving, tracing her fingers lightly over the cave-wall as she danced.

The contractions had begun. After weeks of grumbling pain they had finally begun. They had awoken her a few hours earlier, but knowing she would need all the rest she could get, she had rolled over and somehow managed to fall back to sleep.

She stepped out of the cave, watching as the great orange eye sunk into the ocean. It somehow reminded her of the python - the marks on its back, its opaque pupil, the way it had swallowed the heron. What she had foreseen then - his death - had sustained her these many long months. She doubted if she could have gone through with it if she hadn't known the way he would die. Indeed, the certainty of it had been the deciding factor in their intimacy. A flock of seabirds whirled in the air then settled upon the waves. The sun flattened itself against the horizon. She almost expected to hear a loud sizzling hiss as it boiled into the sea but it disappeared without a sound. She was always glad to see it go.

She looked up at the slab of stone. For once, the cat wasn't there, off on one of its hunting trips. She became a little anxious when the cat wasn't around, particularly at a time like this. She turned around, scanning over the outlines of the cliff and the dark ridges of the range beyond. The moon wasn't up yet and it would be sometime before it soared over the hills. Its pale light would creep over the contours towards her. How she loved that sight. And tonight it would be full. If only it would hurry, she thought, if only it would hurry, just this once.

She stepped back into the cave and stoked the fire into life. She made it larger than usual, placing several thick logs across the flames. The fire crackled enthusiastically - the flames hungry for the logs. She would need a good fire, she told herself as she dusted the dirt from her hands.

A continuous stream of swifts, irritated by the rising smoke, poured out of the cave and into the night. She could feel another contraction beginning.

FIRE IN THE DARKNESS

Mitchell crashed through the undergrowth at a full downhill run. Invisible creatures scuttled out of the way. He had reached such a momentum and the ground beneath him was so slippery that to stop seemed more dangerous than to continue. Occasionally he would brake his descent on the trunks of young saplings, then start again, lurching forward like a wounded bull. At times the gradient was so steep that, without thinking, he threw himself over, feet first, sliding on the leaf-litter and mud until he reached the bottom of the gorge. Charging along the stream beds, leaping from rock to rock, he pictured himself as heroic saviour, the scourge of evil, travelling to the ends of the earth to vanquish the ancient enemy.

He lashed out at the foliage, the short heavy blade of his machete lopping off any branch that ventured too close. Every so often a bundle of cold wet leaves would slap across his face and he would intensify his attack, chopping with renewed vigour at the rank deviant growth.

Even in the pale shadow of moonlight the jungle was too green, too alive for comfort. How he loathed all this luxuriant greenery. He thwacked his way forward, doing his bit to reduce this ungodly corner of the earth to a plain unadorned decency.

In the distance he could hear the roar of a waterfall above the sound of the stream. He plunged on, eager to end this nightmare journey. At last he came to the brink of the cascade and stood there, the mist swirling around him. There in the distance was the coast - the lines of surf crashing against the outcrops. Far below, he could just make out the silvery shapes of the palms as they huddled along the shoreline, like hunchbacks hiding from the moon.

He looked around, suddenly recognising the rock upon which Dominique had sat so many months ago. Swaying like a pendulum, faster and faster, she had been absorbed in the world she'd spun for herself. It was here that he had first realised how unstable she was, and with the western coastline stretching off into the distance, he could now see that it was here that she had first decided to disappear.

Disappearance. He mulled over in his mind what that meant. How everyone he'd ever known, everyone he'd ever been close to, had disappeared, had betrayed him by disappearing. It was inexcusable. He had tried to stop this pattern, tried and failed. And now, if he couldn't stop it, at least he would get on top of it; regain ascendancy, work with it rather than against it, rerun that primal scene a final time. He would come to the rescue and take revenge, all in one. At last, the opportunity was here, to recreate that parallel frame, that image that had bound him all these years and once again step into the film that was his and his alone, that for so long he had been just a spectator of. At last he could unfreeze it, let it roll, and embrace the destiny that for years he had struggled to avoid. He had remained in the passenger seat far too long, watching impassively like the sole-surviving member from a disgruntled audience of his own life. At last he was taking control. He would come to the rescue and - in a curious way - it would be he himself he was rescuing, when all others had proved incapable. That was the beauty of it. And his freedom, his deliverance, would set them all free.

He peered through the curtain of spray at the dark vegetation below, searching for a way down. He climbed over the rocks to the side of the stream and, hanging on to a tree, swung out over the edge. Peering through the moonlit shadows, he could see there was a sheer drop down into the blackness before a steep rocky slope met the tree-line. It was impossible to tell how far down it was. As he swung there, something on a distant headland caught his eye. Obscured by the mist and spray from the falls, he hadn't noticed it before. It was the unmistakable flickering glow of a fire.

He looked at it for a long time, hanging there until his arm began to ache. This was it, he told himself. No question about it. Journey's end in sight. Only the black emptiness below separated them. He closed his eyes, not wanting to waste more time thinking. He let go and dropped into the darkness …

THE BIRTHING MOON

It had intrigued her the way her waters had broken. Humming gently, full of anticipation, she had looked up at the broad face of the moon, and suddenly that was it - they had burst. And so much of it ! She hadn't expected that.

She rested on her bed of *alang-alang* grass and listened to her favourite recordings - waves breaking on the shore, the wind whistling through the limestone. It was soothing to just crouch there, clearing her mind, waiting for the next contraction. Each time the pain came she tried to welcome it; one less to go, she kept telling herself, one less to go. But they had been coming all night long and she was starting to tire.

She'd been determined not to let the pain get to

her and now she was pleased that so far it hadn't. In fact, it seemed to have stopped. Nothing at all had happened for some time now and it was beginning to worry her.

The moon had finally crept into that part of the sky she called her own and its pale light now flooded through the arched mouth of the cave, soft and restful.

She stretched out on the dry grasses and toyed with the idea of catching some sleep.

The sudden, tremendous downwards urge was so insistent, so forceful that she was completely taken aback. She crawled out of bed and braced herself against the rock-wall, gasping for breath. The sharpness of the pain, the intensity, was so unsparing, so shocking that she found herself groaning out loud.

She heard the sound of her own groans as if from far away. Yet despite the pain, a part of her was revelling in the power of the experience. She loved the sheer out-of-control feeling, the overwhelming sense of being unable to do anything - anything at all - to change the process. Trust - that was what she had always been seeking; someone or something to trust. And here it was, finally. Here was something she could give in to without fear; and she had no choice - that was what made it so different, special - she had no control over what was happening - it was bigger than her, it was the power of life itself.

The pain subsided momentarily and then was back again, stronger, more intense than before. Any moment now - she could feel it - any moment now. She crouched lower, ready to hold the child as it came out.

She was sure she could hear movement from the entrance of the cave. At last, she thought, at last the cat has returned. It had been away so long now that she had grown worried.

Suddenly, the pain, the urgency, the unstoppable downward pressure were all converging towards one final searing moment. She looked up and saw him there, framed in the entranceway, the cat perched above him, ready to pounce. Perfect, she thought, as a long excruciating scream filled the cavern. She looked down, cradling the child's head, the blood trickling between her fingers. Out of the corner of her eye she could see the panther, its eyes gleaming, tearing her father limb from limb.

THE TRIANGULAR SAIL

He had found the cave with little trouble. The tell-tale wisps of smoke from the headland had led him straight to it. Yet despite this, he could see why Dominique had chosen the site. Miles from the lighthouse, along a stretch of coastline that no one ever visited, in a part of the reserve where regular patrols were non-existent, it was a perfect hideout.

The fire was still burning by the time he'd climbed the spur. He had seen the curious scuffles in the sand; the random patterns, the splashes of blood that hadn't quite congealed. He'd followed them out of the cave along the path, down through the forest, into an extraordinary circular area of cultivation, as symmetrical as a web. And there in the middle he had found him, buried up to his chin, his head bruised and swollen, planted like a coconut in the fresh jungle loam.

He had been astonished to discover that the cameraman was still alive; a faint breath fluttering from his nostrils. Frantically, like a man possessed, he'd started digging with his bare hands.

"Mitchell !" he screamed, throwing handfuls of earth up behind him. In a way that he couldn't explain, his life had become inextricably tied to Mitchell's. It seemed imperative to save him. He raced down to the stream to fill the water bottle, scrambling back over the rocks as fast as he could.

Bending down, he cradled Mitchell's head and held the bottle above his blackened lips, pouring the water over his face and open mouth, desperate to revive him. It ran down the cameraman's chin, glistening on his blood-caked bristles, a dark stain soaking slowly into the soil.

"Mitchell," he whispered, breathing softly into his ear. He was holding the battered head with a quiet reverence, as if attempting to germinate the sole-surviving seed of a rare, previously unknown species.

"Mitchell, I know you can hear me ..."

The humidity, the warmth, the waves of insect sound, all seemed to converge in the noonday glare.

Slowly, almost imperceptibly, Mitchell's mouth opened a little, a low nearly inaudible groan escaping from his lips.

"Mitchell…"

The natural amphitheatre of the garden concentrated the tropical heat like an oven.

"Mitchell … breathe … breathe deeply …"

He watched as Mitchell's breath seemed to slow, become a little more rhythmic.

Half-spluttering, half-groaning, Mitchell's face lurched suddenly forward, his eyes rolling open. That same gaze stared up at him, the gaze that had haunted him for so long: defiant, obsessed, now ebbing away.

"The child …"

"I know about the child, Mitchell. Don't worry … I'll get you out of here ..."

"She said ..."

He looked into the yellowing eyes. He could see the life slipping away.

"She said …"

The sound of the insects seemed to intensify as he strained to hear.

Mitchell's breathing was again distant, erratic.

"... was yours ..."

He found himself nodding.

"Yes ... I guessed." He remembered that last night before she had left for the airport. That certainty had been what had driven him these last few weeks. Hearing Mitchell say it somehow completed everything, the three of them now woven into a shape he could recognise. Yet he wondered if they would ever really know the truth and whether this parting shot had been Dominique's final revenge. He could see the sense of disappointment on the cameraman's face, the look of resigned defeat, as if there was now nothing left to live for. Carefully, he once again bathed Mitchell's disfigured features, pouring the water over the worst of the wounds with a gentleness that surprised him.

"Just keep breathing, Mitchell ..."

The man who had left him in the swamp no longer existed. Keeping him alive was all that mattered. A natural reverence for life and for the life before him welled up within him, dispelling the last remaining shards of anger as effortlessly as daylight dispelling darkness. It occurred to him that compassion was the most natural human state and all other feelings and thoughts obscured this simple truth.

He dug into the dark soil, exposing the torn flesh and gaping wounds. Leaf-mould and congealed blood covered the cameraman's shoulders. Claw marks shredded their way across his back and chest. What was left of his arm dangled raw at his side.

Unsupported for a moment, Mitchell's head had fallen to his chest and his eyes had again half-opened. A dreadful drawn-out croak escaped from between his lips. His breath had stopped. Grabbing Mitchell's chin, Villiers blew into his mouth. He could feel the muscles twitching. He blew again and again. The cameraman's eyelids flickered briefly but after a while it was clear he was dead.

* * *

Now, sitting on the beach, he watched the small triangle of canvas as it headed for the south point. In a few minutes it would disappear around the headland. He had first seen it from the ridge above Dominique's garden and had rushed back down to the beach, racing along the shoreline towards it. It hadn't been long before he'd spotted the tracks - he knew they were hers - the single tracks of light well-made boots, and followed them to the spot where they were met by a larger group of footprints - four men, four familiar sets of footprints - down to the shoreline where they'd pushed the shallow-hulled boat out into the surf.

The triangular sail was now approaching the headland. Buffeted by the strong sou'wester blowing around the point, the entire rig heeled suddenly downwards then was righted as the crew once more gained control. Tacking into the wind, the poacher's tiny craft looked for one moment as if it might never round the point. The thought flashed across his mind that he might outrun it, scramble around the rocks, and somehow convince them to let her go. Then suddenly the boat slipped behind the headland and was gone.

He sat there, watching the spot, the salt spray blowing around his ears. The seagulls wheeled raucously above the waves. He fingered the chunk of volcanic glass he'd found on the cave-floor, washing it in the rock pool at his feet. He reached up, feeling the patch of linen across his eye. He took it off, examining it with his one good eye, reading the streaks of mucus, blood and pus as if they were some augury of the future, some map of what he had to do next. He folded it neatly and placed it down on the rocks. He touched his eyelids, gently pushing his fingers into the softness between. Gradually, with great care, he loosened the rotting flesh that still clung to his skull. He was surprised how little it hurt, as if all that he'd been through, all the broken dreams and dashed hopes had in some way anaesthetised him against feeling any further pain. Using the chunk of obsidian, he cut through the last stubborn ligaments and optical tissues, then, pushing in his forefinger, he positioned it until he was ready. With one final movement he pulled out the eye, tossing it to the foaming surf.

The gulls swooped and dived along the breakers.

He bent down, washing the empty socket and bandage in the saline waters of the pool.

When he had finished he stood up. If he ran hard, he could be back at the lighthouse in a little under two hours. He knew that once motoring in the Coast Guard launch, it wouldn't take long to overhaul the poacher's boat.

THE ARRIVAL

The boat perched precariously at the top of a wave, crashing down into the trough with a thump. Dominique looked down at the tiny face cradled in her arms. It was beautiful. It seemed so old, so wise; yet it was so new. She studied the soft line of its hair, looking down over the full noble shape of the forehead to the upturned button of its nose and the gorgeous mouth - curved like the bow of an archer and ever-so-slightly smiling. It seemed that all the wisdom, all the compassion, all the beauty in existence had come to rest in that face. She lifted the cotton shawl and peeked once again at the little body, protecting it from the salt-spray with her arm. It was just as he had pictured it in her mind, perfect in every detail.

Once again, the boat rolled up the crest of a wave, lurching uneasily down the other side. From out here, on the open sea, the hills of the reserve seemed small and far away, enshrouded in a pale blue mist. She was glad to be leaving.

Pointing furiously in a particular direction, one of the poachers was shouting instructions to the helmsman. She turned and for the first time saw the shape of a larger boat, a launch, bearing fast towards them. Onboard, the dark silhouette of a machine-gun crouched above the bow. Agile figures were running along its deck.

The helmsman steered the boat away from it, towards the next headland. He smiled unpleasantly at her, his teeth protruding in a yellow tobacco-stained grin. Just a few feet away, he seemed to inhabit a different world - a world she was leaving behind, as distant from her and the child as it was possible to get. Yet she knew that she was safe now, safe at last from all that lay behind her. Ahead lay only the future, and although she could no longer see it as clearly, it held no fear for her.

It had all been worth it.

She looked down again at the child. It lay there, its eyes half-open, staring back at her, as if posing some unanswerable question about the situation in which it now found itself. Between its legs, its tiny penis pointed skyward, and beneath it, perfectly formed, she could see the bud-like shape of its female sex. She had always known it would be like this. It was such a relief to see her vision fulfilled and the child's hermaphrodite nature safely delivered.

It was only the beginning, she told herself, an evolutionary step forward that held undreamt of possibilities. In the years to come, more and more would arrive, the special ones, torchbearers for a new species. They would multiply. They would flourish. She felt privileged to be a part of it.

The sound of the launch's engine was louder now. She looked up and saw that it was almost upon them. He was there, standing in the bow like she knew he would be, his arms outstretched as he gripped the railing, his eye-patch blazing in the sun.

She would have to find some other way of leaving him.

www.ingramcontent.com/pod-product-compliance
Lightning Source LLC
Chambersburg PA
CBHW030816310726
48980CB00006B/521/J

* 9 7 8 0 9 5 6 5 2 5 4 0 6 *